"You need time from the memories, Megan," Gerard said. "You need someone to listen. Help. Support."

"And that would be you, of course."

"Exactly. Have the nightmares stopped since you arrived here?"

Megan turned away. "Please, I'm not ready for this. I can't—" She shoved away from the post. There was the sadness again, not only in her eyes, but in every inch of her body.

"Kirstie told me about her blackouts," Gerard said. "Did she mention to you that she was afraid she was being poisoned?"

Megan's expression froze, her eyes darkened with shock. "She told you that? Why didn't she say something to me about it?"

"You refused to take her case."

"Of course I did. She needs a neurologist."

Gerard shook his head. "You still think that?"

Megan raised an elegantly arched brow. "What would you say if I told you she warned me recently that I could be in danger?"

Books by Hannah Alexander

Love Inspired Suspense

*Note of Peril
*Under Suspicion
*Death Benefits
Hidden Motive
Season of Danger
  "Silent Night, Deadly Night"
Eye of the Storm

Love Inspired Historical

*Hideaway Home

Love Inspired Single Title

*Hideaway
*Safe Haven
*Last Resort
*Fair Warning
*Grave Risk
*Double Blind
A Killing Frost
**Sacred Trust
**Silent Pledge
**Solemn Oath

*Hideaway
**Sacred Trust

HANNAH ALEXANDER

is the pseudonym of husband-and-wife writing team Cheryl and Mel Hodde (pronounced "Hoddee"). When they first met, Mel had just begun his new job as an E.R. doctor in Cheryl's hometown, and Cheryl was working on a novel. Cheryl's matchmaking pastor set them up on an unexpected blind date at a local restaurant. Surprised by the sneak attack, Cheryl blurted the first thing that occurred to her: "You're a doctor? Could you help me paralyze someone?" Mel was shocked. "Only temporarily, of course," she explained when she saw his expression. "And only fictiously. I'm writing a novel."

They began brainstorming immediately. Eighteen months later they were married, and the novels they set in fictitious Ozark towns began to sell. The first novel in the Hideaway series won the prestigious Christy Award for Best Romance in 2004.

HANNAH ALEXANDER

EYE *of the* STORM

Love Inspired

Recycling programs
for this product may
not exist in your area.

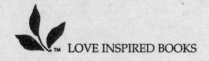

LOVE INSPIRED BOOKS

ISBN-13: 978-0-373-44480-9

EYE OF THE STORM

www.LoveInspiredBooks.com

Printed in U.S.A.

He stilled the storm to a whisper;
the waves of the sea were hushed.
—*Psalms* 107:29

Eye of the Storm is dedicated to
the Jolly Mill Park Foundation, a group of people
who unselfishly give of their time, energy
and finances to keep Jolly Mill Park active
and remind us of its fascinating history.
We very much appreciate the permission we were
given to bring the tiny town of Jolly Mill alive
and populate it with more buildings, more people,
more suspense than typically takes place in this
beautiful setting. Readers are wholeheartedly
invited to come visit the real Jolly Mill and explore
reminders of its long history. Prepare for a taste
of the actual history of this town in upcoming
historical titles about the Village of Jollification.

ONE

A silver blade sliced through the curtained exam room, its target the helpless patient of Dr. Megan Bradley. The hand that held the blade was crusted with grime, fingernails whitening as it squeezed the handle with the force of fury. Megan clutched the cold steel of a revolver in her hand, aimed it at the faceless attacker's chest and pulled the trigger.

No burst came from the chamber. No sound touched her at all. She tried to scream. Silence. The blade reflected Megan's contorted features as it plunged downward again. The pressure of her scream threatened to explode from her chest. She fought her way out of the silent nightmare of a Corpus Christi rescue mission clinic and into her soft bed in the darkness of her tiny cabin in the Missouri woods.

"No!" She battled the blankets and sat up, still seeing the sweet, dark-haired young homeless woman with the huge belly. "Oh, Joni, no."

Megan squeezed her eyes shut at the hideous memory that repeated itself far too often at night...the killer ripping his way through the curtained cubicle...the blood... the screams mingling with the recoil of Megan's weapon as the loud report deafened her. She watched the grimy killer hit the floor, splattering blood and ripping a section of the curtain from the ceiling. And then she slid through the blood to Joni's side to find the young woman's eyes staring into nothing.

Gerard Vance rushed into the ruined cubicle, his head brushing the rails that held the curtain, his shoulders framing him as he entered. At the sight of Joni, his face filled with grim pain. He dropped to his knees at Megan's side without a glance at the dead man tangled in the fallen curtain. "I've got your back, Megan. Don't look at him. Let's get the baby out."

With his aid, Megan held her tears and controlled her hands, performing a postmortem C-section, sickened by the desecration of her sweet young patient's body. The cry of little Daria, Joni's orphan, soon filled the clinic, the sound of life echoing past her young mother's death.

Megan forced away the malignant memory, forced herself to breathe slowly, forced her eyes to open. She brushed the hair from her face and focused on her surroundings, anything but the reason she'd fled Corpus Christi. A slight breeze outside moved a tree branch across the window beside her bed—a lifeline to reality. A trickle of moisture drew her fingers to her neck; she touched the droplets of perspiration.

She blinked slowly and in that brief moment she was attacked once more by the memory of her own contorted features in the killer's knife blade, like a misshapen mirror. The dregs of the nightmare mingled with reality.

She flung the blanket from her legs and leapt from the bed. "Wake up," she muttered into the chilly one-room cabin. "Stop this. You're doing it to yourself, Megan."

Talking to herself, yes, but even the sound of her own voice helped break the spell. Inhaling deeply and then exhausting her lungs of air, as if she could cleanse her system of the weight of knowledge with the carbon dioxide, she kept her attention on the movement of that one branch outside the nearest window. Though gray in the night, she knew she would see the green color of life when the sun rose. Focus on the hope of dawn.

"It isn't happening," she whispered into the cool air. "Not now. It's over." The nightmare receded with great reluctance, but left behind emptiness. How long would she live with these terrors?

Distracted at last by the gray-and-black silk of nighttime in the forest, Megan sank back onto the bed. The softness of the mattress reproached her despite the good intentions of Kirstie and Lynley Marshal, the dear friends who had furnished this hideaway for her two weeks ago. Her patient, Joni Park, was relegated to the grave, separated from her baby forever. What had the surviving doctor done to deserve such luxury?

"I failed," Megan whispered to the room. All those months she'd carried a weapon to protect the helpless, but when a knife ripped through that curtained enclosure, she'd been unable to do a thing. There'd simply been no warning.

The peeping of tree frogs drifted in through the mass of windows in the cottage's front wall. Megan willed the sound to wash over her and clear away the hovering menace. These were safe Missouri sounds, not the setting of her recurrent dreams. It was a rent-free cottage just past the outskirts of the village of Jolly Mill, near the bank of Capps Creek. So why did she continue to dwell in that hot place of dread every night when she closed her eyes?

Cool air chilled the moisture of her skin; her shivering returned, this time as much from cold as from lingering memories. She stood up again, allowing her bare feet to conform to the ridges of the old wooden floor before she checked the lighted numbers of the alarm clock. It was five in the morning. Upon her return to her childhood home-town, she'd put an end to her practice of rising before the sun and studying her latest medical journals or a new text-book.

She'd put an end to several old habits, hoping the change would bring about at least the impression of heal-ing. Nothing worked. Old habits didn't like to be aban-doned. Though her sleep aid had gotten her through the past two weeks, last night's dose seemed to have devel-oped a shorter half-life.

Her heart continued its tachycardic rhythm. She pulled on her warm terry robe, rubbing her arms with her hands as she stepped to the multi-paned window in the front door of the cottage. How many times since Joni's murder had she considered getting therapy?

But shouldn't she know the drill after working with so many patients at the Vance Rescue Mission? She wasn't living on the street or battling psychosis or alcoholism or drug addiction. Couldn't she work this out for herself?

Still, the foreboding persisted as every creak of the cot-tage, every odd sound outside, instead of comforting her, sent a fresh chill through her. Maybe resuming her habit of early-morning study would be a good distraction.

She stepped around the red antique room divider, tugging the collar of her robe more closely around her neck as she glanced around the room. The furnishings so generously provided to her by her tiny group of long-time girlfriends were barely outlined by the gentle glow of moonlight that drifted down through the treetops and through the windows.

She went to the kitchenette for a drink of water, her shadow faint against the sand-colored walls of the one-room cottage—a hue that reminded her too much of the place from which she'd fled.

Megan seldom concerned herself with the appearance of her surroundings. The recent flurry of decorating—the red divider, the Roman shades over the multiple windows across the front of the cottage—had been Kirstie Marshal's idea. When thinking clearly, Kirstie was good with a hammer and screwdriver. The love seat in the tiny sitting area had come from Nora Thompson's own home. This cottage was Thompson property.

As a teenager, Megan once dreamed of living in this very cottage, so deep in the woods, so isolated from the world…but of course, not far from Alec Thompson, the boy she'd had a crush on since fifth grade. Most times, she loved the peace of this place. Though Alec no longer lived in the family home with his mother, Megan took comfort in knowing that Nora was still barely two hundred yards through the woods in the big house on the cliff above the creek.

Five in the morning, however, wasn't a good time to call Nora to come running down the hill with hot cocoa and a dozen of her famous black walnut–butterscotch cookies. Megan saw Jolly Mill as a place of comfort, but she also saw it as personal failure. She hadn't even been able to face a full two years of real life in the trenches.

Here, everyone in town knew her by her first, middle and last names, and some could recall the subject of her valedictorian speech on graduation night. She had old friends and classmates who'd lingered in Jolly Mill to carry on the family businesses, to settle with their own families and continue a long tradition of farming. They weren't hiding here—they were living here.

She was hiding.

The sleeping pill had made her thirsty during the night, and she swigged down the whole glass of water and poured another, listening to the music of the peepers and the breeze that gently rustled through the spring leaves outside. The faint sound of a small motor kicking on in the pump house to replace the water she'd poured. It kicked off just as quickly.

A quiet melody took its place and it took her a few seconds to recognize the tone of her new cell phone. It grew louder as she listened, shooting through the cottage. She stiffened. A phone call in the dark had always been her least favorite sound.

Her legs felt stiff as she rushed to the phone, then answered and peered out at the foggy, moonlit haven that surrounded the cottage.

"Lynley?"

"Thank goodness." Her best friend's voice, normally brisk and filled with energy, sounded tight and raspy through the receiver.

"What is it?"

"Mom's disappeared again and this time I haven't been able to find her."

Megan turned from the window. No. Not again. Poor Kirstie. "How long has she been missing?"

"Maybe all night. I can't believe I didn't check on her, but she was doing so well the past few days and I was studying late. I remember laughing with her because she teased me about what she should call me when I got my doctorate in nursing. She named me Dr. Nurse Marshal. I was tired and I thought she'd gone to bed, and I fell asleep—"

"Lynley, calm down," Megan said. "Call some neighbors and ask them to help search. She may have taken shelter in a barn again until it gets light enough for her to find her way home."

"I've already called everyone whose land adjoins ours. No one's found her. I know they're getting tired of my calls, though Elmer Batschelet offered to use his dogs to track her. I'll probably take him up on it if she doesn't show up soon. Do you know how many times this has happened in the past month?"

Megan took her lower lip between her teeth. Now was not the time for recriminations, but couldn't Lynley see the obvious? "This makes the second since I've arrived." An average of once a week.

"It's getting worse."

"Have you called the sheriff?" Megan asked.

"He and his men are out searching. Again. Poor Sheriff Moritz. And poor Mom. She's always so embarrassed when this happens."

"We can help her deal with the embarrassment later. First get her safely home." Megan stretched. "When she shows up, bring her by the clinic so we can check her out."

"I'll be in for work as soon as I find her." There was a sigh. "If I do. If she's okay. I doubt she'll be in shape to even answer phones today."

Megan allowed those statements to linger. Maybe Lynley would talk herself into doing the right thing and prevent a quarrel that neither of them wanted right now. Kirstie's daughter needed to see reason before Kirstie got hurt.

"Megan?" The voice was tentative, almost as if Lynley could hear Megan's thoughts. And she probably could. They'd known each other from the cradle. "What if she doesn't come back this time?"

Instead of reassuring her friend as she had been doing since Kirstie's mysterious episodes began last month, Megan pressed her lips together. It was a good question. Maybe Lynley needed to follow it to its logical conclusion and start dealing with the dangers of her state of denial.

"Megan?"

"I don't know, but you can't keep trying to do this alone." Megan felt awful as she spoke the words, but as Kirstie herself had said, her daughter wouldn't listen to reason. "You need help."

"We just need to get through this until we figure out what's really causing the problem."

Megan forced a gentleness to her voice. "Then if you won't accept help, place her into protection until we do get it figured out."

"Protection?" There was a soft snort. "You mean imprison her, don't you?"

"I mean arrange it so this doesn't happen again."

"Megan, she's a vital, active, fifty-two-year-old woman, not someone accustomed to sitting in a rocking chair or being cooped up in a block of rooms. You think she deserves to be locked up in a nursing home?"

"I don't think she deserves Alzheimer's, but—"

"Don't say that! I hate that word. You know as soon as that diagnosis is made and the patient is shoved into a lockdown ward, no one ever searches for other causes, they just treat the symptoms. I'm not giving up on her that easily."

"I'm not telling you to give up."

"This isn't sundowner's syndrome."

Megan couldn't miss the increasing tautness of Lynley's voice. "It's okay," she told her friend. "You're not alone in this. I'm here for you."

There was a brief silence and then "How? You wouldn't move in with us."

Shame attacked Megan. She didn't have the strength to explain yet. "I'll do all I can to help you and Kirstie through it."

"You mean help Dr. Kelsey convince us she really is

losing her mind?" There was a plaintive sadness in Lynley's words.

Megan closed her eyes. "I didn't say that. I'm here as your friend."

There was a quiet sigh. "Okay. Thanks. I'm glad you're back in Jolly Mill even if we don't agree about everything."

"We've never agreed about everything."

"This is different."

"Can't you just trust me for once? I am a doctor now."

"And I'm a nurse. So is Mom."

"So you're saying two nurses trump a doctor?" Megan forced a smile so it would bleed into her voice. Anything to lighten the moment.

"Something like that. Megan, are you…" She paused, sighed. "Be honest with me. Why did you come back here?"

Megan closed her eyes. There it was. The question.

"Your family's all in Cape Girardeau now," Lynley continued. "Why didn't you go there? Not that I didn't want you to come here, because I did, but—"

"You should know why. This is still home to me." Unlike being with her family. If she heard Mom tell her one more time how wonderful it was to have grandchildren, and that she wanted more, Megan would pledge lifelong celibacy. Let her big brother provide all the descendants for the Bradley family. Randy seemed happy to do it.

"Megan," Lynley said, "did Mom ask you to come here and convince me to let her check into a nursing facility?"

Megan hesitated a second too long. "That's not why I came."

"But she did ask you."

"She's afraid you'll waste the rest of your life taking care of—"

"Waste? Did you say waste?"

"She's the one who said it, Lynley, not me."

"Careful, or you'll begin to sound like Dad."

"Notice I actually came to Jolly Mill. I didn't leave," Megan snapped. *Unlike your father,* she wanted to say, but Lynley knew what she meant. Barry Marshal was a self-centered egotist who had split soon after Kirstie's Alzheimer's diagnosis. For everyone's sake, he should have split long before that. Megan knew too many of that man's secrets. Too many Jolly Mill secrets.

"Sorry," Lynley said. "You're right. I know."

"Just bring Kirstie to the office *when* you find her," Megan said.

"I will. Thanks."

"I can come help you search."

"No. You just be there for us when I find her." That slender edge of tension lingered after Lynley disconnected. Megan knew her friend's resentment wasn't directed totally at her. She was just the punching bag for all Lynley was going through, for all Barry's failures as a father. Megan wasn't taking punches very well right now. Lynley didn't know about Joni's murder. No one here did.

Kirstie would be found again—or she would return herself home when she regained her senses, as she had done every time she'd gone missing. Everyone in the Jolly Mill community knew her and watched out for her.

Megan pushed her cell phone back into her deep purse and was turning back toward bed when a flash of light struck one of the panes. Brief. Barely there.

She frowned, staring out into the darkness. Had she actually seen that, or was it a side effect of her sleeping pill? The drug could do strange things to some people. She'd considered more than once the possibility that the drugs were causing the dreams, but she'd so craved sleep after the weeks of sleeplessness following Joni's murder that she took them anyway.

A whisper of a different kind reached her from outside—not wind or frogs or the sound of the electric water pump. There was another flash. A newly familiar strum of panic restricted Megan's feet to the woven mat by the front door.

She clenched her fists. *Don't allow the panic to control you.* This wasn't the mean streets of the city. This was tiny Jolly Mill, safe, quiet, secluded. She didn't need a weapon here to protect herself.

Another sound reached her—tires crunching on rock?

Her fear quickened. When she entered her drive, her tires always met the gravel on the quarter-mile track that led to this cottage. What she'd just heard might be that gravel pop-snap in the distance. Maybe someone had turned around at the mailbox and was driving away. That had to be it.

The only sounds she typically heard here at night were the occasional bark of a farm dog, the lowing of a cow separated from her calf or the spine-tingling call of an owl that sounded more like mocking laughter at her plight. None of the wildlife in this area sounded like a car.

As she wavered, the soft rumble grew louder, followed by a flicker of shadows through the trees. A vehicle. An aura of stealth seemed to fill and then illuminate the darkness like a hunter stalking its prey.

The drive to this cottage was private. No one else around here had reason to be on it at this time of morning—except maybe a patient in trouble? She'd decided not to have a landline, despite the spotty cell coverage in Jolly Mill. If there was an urgent medical need, it was feasible someone could be coming for help, though there was a hospital in Monett less than twenty minutes away and in Cassville only a little farther in the other direction.

She checked the dead bolt lock on the front door. Of course she'd locked it. The past few years had taught her that. No one had ever locked the doors when she was growing up in Jolly Mill. Something else people seldom did was close the curtains, but right now lowering the Roman shades over all the windows seemed like a good idea.

The tight cords bit into her hands as she jerked them down, one by one. Her movements double-timed as lights crested the hill and shot through the tiny cracks in the woven material. The sharp, quick sound of her breath was harsh as it hit the matted shades. This was no dream. One set of cords tangled together, the shades tilting drunkenly as she worked a knot free and straightened the bottom edge. She rushed to the next window and then the next until she had a pseudo-barrier from the onslaught of light.

Megan's suddenly overactive imagination transformed her little patch of wooded paradise into a battleground. Even as she castigated herself for her fear, she could do nothing to ease it.

Calm. Stay calm. Joni's killer is dead. There's no one after you. She wouldn't call for help just because of a car approaching the house. She didn't need anyone in town to think the doctor at the new clinic was unhinged. But who was coming here? Mom and Dad would have called if they were planning a trip across the state, and they wouldn't have driven all night to get here.

Megan retreated into the shadows of the far corner of the sitting area. She curled into the love seat, clutching the throw pillow to her chest as she waited.

The holy scent reached her from the homemade sachet

her former Sunday school teacher had sewn into the pillow. Martha Irene called it one of her "prayer pillows," but Megan couldn't pray. Who would hear her? She just squeezed the cushion hard against her chest and tried to slow her panicked imagination while the rhythm of her heart encroached on the chambers of her lungs.

She should definitely have sought treatment for PTSD.

The vehicle lights went off and the engine died, plunging her into dark silence for another few seconds before she heard a door opening and then footsteps brushing through unmown grass and last year's leaves. There was a soft sound of someone stepping onto her wooden front porch and then a pause while she tried to still her panicked breathing, fingernails digging into her hands. This was crazy. If someone wanted to hurt her, they wouldn't approach this way. And yet she hadn't been totally rational since arriving here. Everything was still too fresh, and the dreams each night reminded her that the world was a dangerous place.

No one knocked. There was no doorbell. The pain in her hands distracted her.

A familiar voice reached her. One word, softly spoken. "Megan."

She silently gulped in a great lungful of air. It couldn't be.

"Megan? It's me. Gerard."

She stared through the darkness toward the door, and at once her fear metamorphosed into something even less manageable. How dare Gerard Vance follow her here?

TWO

Gerard didn't want to knock. "Megan, please." He could hear the cracking fatigue in his own voice. Could she hear it too?

According to his late-sleeping sister, Tess, who'd taken a couple of road trips with Megan last year, Megan had never slept this late when she lived in Corpus Christi. In fact, Tess complained that Megan never even allowed the sun to rise before her on a day off.

He knew she was here because as he'd driven up his headlights had flashed across her bright yellow Neo parked beneath the limbs of a huge oak tree around back—no missing that color. Megan was nothing if not safety-conscious. When he'd helped her pick out a replacement car last year after her old one breathed its last, her only requirement was a bright color. The front window of the car was illuminated by a few streaks of moonlight that filtered through the leaves.

"Megan, I'm not going away. I may camp out here until daylight, but I'm not leaving."

He waited. Nothing. No movement inside at all.

Hadn't he seen light coming through the windows a moment ago? It may have been a reflection, or imagination…though Gerard didn't give in easily to imagination.

He pressed his forehead against the door frame of the tiny cottage. No one answered as he continued to wait. No light came on.

That didn't mean Megan was asleep. It could just mean she was turning a deaf ear to his voice outside her front door, as she'd ignored the messages he'd left on her cell and at the clinic this past week...and with Kirstie Marshal, his source.

The energy that had kept him going for the past twenty-four hours—a full day at the mission followed by a long night of driving—began to wane. He was here. He couldn't force Megan to open the door or to answer him, but he still had to find some way to breach the divide for her sake and, selfishly, for his. His clinic needed her, and though several local docs in the Corpus Christi area had volunteered to fill in during her absence, she'd developed a bond with her patients. She'd developed a bond with him, and he wasn't about to let that be destroyed.

"Look," he said, more softly still. "I'm not here to nag you about your work ethic, okay?" She still owed three months out of two years of work at the rescue mission clinic for her med school loans. She needed to complete those months. He was pretty sure she would be given some leeway by the loan officer, considering her trauma, he just didn't know how much.

Unfortunately, he'd tried to point out that she could be jeopardizing her career if she left when she did. He'd learned the hard way that she didn't respond to authority very well. Why had he made that stupid mistake after he'd known her for twenty-one months—appearing to pull rank on her as she'd walked away from the clinic? Demanding she fulfill her obligation? Sometimes he behaved like an inexperienced young buck. Desperation did that to him on occasion, especially when it came to a certain irresistible doctor with a mind of her own.

"Megan, are you studying?"

She'd often teased him about taking a detour past her apartment every morning on his way to the mission just to check up on her. How could he help it? He liked being near her, even if just in the neighborhood. The sight of her cheerful smile, the warmth in those golden-brown eyes, evident for all patients to see, had grabbed Gerard by the scruff of the heart as they had the rest of the staff.

It had taken his sister, Tess, to point out that Megan, with the long curtain of wavy hair the color of ginger, the delicate yet audaciously feminine lines of face and body— Tess's description, not his—could win an international beauty contest. What he knew of Dr. Megan Bradley's heart affected him more than any physical beauty.

And now, after nearly two years spent helping the neediest of patients, she was the one in need of help. Gerard held himself responsible for the tragedy at the clinic three weeks ago, and he couldn't allow Megan to isolate herself out here in the woods because of it.

Of course, he was probably being egocentric to think that she belonged at the mission clinic permanently, that her life should revolve around his calling. He'd not been mistaken, however, about the look in her eyes these past few months as they met together about her patients. She loved them.

Had he been mistaken to think she was looking forward to his company with as much enthusiasm as he was to hers? Was he imagining that she cared for him? The shock of Joni Park's murder had destroyed more than Joni's life. It had shaken the foundations of everyone her life had touched, and though Joni's sister was devastated, Megan had been the one to bear firsthand witness to the destruction of the young woman's body.

The boards squeaked beneath his feet as he turned to gaze out into the dark morning and rested his head against the support post. It was possible Megan had changed her routine since leaving Corpus Christi. She may still be sleeping. It was possible.

His eyes closed of their own will. Such a long trip... but he'd made it for so many good reasons. Tess and Sean could run the mission until he returned. Gerard had things to attend to here in Jolly Mill.

Tree frogs slowed their croaking and fell silent. A tractor started up in the distance and a rooster crowed at the stars...or perhaps at the vague lightening of the darkness past the tree line. There was a rustle of brush nearby and a cottontail rabbit hopped across the overgrown lawn, sniffing for an early breakfast. Gerard stepped down from the porch and felt the soft cushion of grass beneath his shoes as he returned to the car. Once inside he closed the door quietly so he wouldn't awaken Megan—if she truly was asleep and not just waiting for him to leave. He moved the back of his seat to nearly horizontal and closed his eyes.

Morning was here, though the sky had not yet turned blue, and the sun had not yet penetrated the forest. He would allow the gray darkness to hold him in sleep for a few moments, but Megan would not be able to leave this place without speaking to him.

Megan sat frozen on the love seat as rips tore through the protective emotional screen of forgetfulness and Gerard's deep voice echoed in her mind. A new kind of fear controlled her thoughts. Why had he come when he must know how hard she was trying to forget?

How could the founder and director of a rescue mis-

sion be so demanding? He expected too much. Anger, her
constant companion, thrummed through her. How dare
he traipse up here after her? This was *her* home, her safe
place. She needed this respite.

She inhaled the scent in her pillow, as she had so many
times these past two weeks to counter the scent of blood
that had fixed itself in her memory. Why had she tried to
convince herself that it was even possible to forget? Gerard
Vance would have to realize that she couldn't match his
psychological strength. This was what she got for trying.
Nightmares.

Would he ever be able to understand that? The man had
a vocation that was the passion of his life, and he would
ride roughshod over anyone who stood in his way. He'd
made that obvious when she left.

Megan's fingers dug into the prayer pillow as images
tumbled past her carefully set barriers: that wicked blade,
Joni's wide, frightened eyes, terror giving way to pain, the
echo of screams that continued to pursue Megan through
the dark passages of her dreams—and now Gerard Vance
following behind her, making his demands like some kind
of Viking warrior.

How could she return to work in that place that bore the
permanent imprint of brutality, and why was he camped
outside her house?

With a sigh, she got up and tiptoed to the front door.
She peered through the wooden slats at the car in her
drive. The front driver's seat was not in evidence, which
meant the blond-haired giant was most likely trying to
sleep in a very cramped and uncomfortable position. A
rush of unwanted tenderness swept through her before
she could disengage from it. Imposing in size and appearance, Gerard Vance was an intimidating man, and he was
a missionary. Incongruous. She'd grown up believing that

missionaries and ministers had to be warm and gentle and tender with everyone all the time.

Typical for Gerard, he flew in the face of convention. He'd thrown many a troublemaker out onto the sidewalk for one false move in the shelter, and he'd done it single-handedly. He'd been nearly as tough on her when she'd left the mission to come here. Gerard didn't have to call for police backup very often. An ex-cop knew how to handle himself.

As she watched, he rose from the seat, as if he had some supernatural way of knowing she was watching him. He looked straight toward her as if he knew she'd be peering at him from this very place. She stepped back, impatient with herself, a grown woman running back home to escape life, hiding to avoid a conversation she didn't want to have.

But she'd tried to face this in Corpus Christi and the continuing despair had nearly destroyed her. She couldn't go back there and didn't have what it took to argue with him this morning. Strange how the thought of not returning to her patients felt like losing a piece of herself. Especially strange since the thought of returning terrified her so badly she couldn't function.

She changed from her nightgown into jeans and her favorite green flannel shirt. Hearing Gerard's voice had reminded her how much she missed her friends in Corpus Christi, but each time she thought of them her memories bore down on her with the thud of a bass drum. Were Tess and Sean still planning a wedding, or had they chucked it all and decided to elope? And Gerard…what was he doing for a full-time doctor in the clinic? Was he interviewing for prospective replacements, or was he waiting for her to return? Did he miss her?

It was impossible not to think about him—his piercing blue eyes, the short blond hair that spiked in the moist breeze from the shore, the firm chin and the gravel of his voice. Those were only the outer characteristics of a man with more of an inner-thought life than any minister or professor of philosophy she'd ever known. He had such a capacity to care for the unlovable. A woman couldn't spend nearly two years working with a man like that and not have an impression of him left on her soul.

Gerard Vance was the kind of man who left an impression on everyone who met him, particularly those who had no homes, no livelihood, and depended on him for the very food they ate and the beds in which they slept.

Reluctantly summoning her courage, Megan stepped out onto the front porch and heard the sound of a car door closing. She looked up to see Gerard walking across the yard, wearing his typical jeans and T-shirt—today the shirt was tie-dyed blue and white. His hair appeared more blond, slightly longer, his skin more tanned than when she'd left him standing at the shelter two weeks ago.

She met his gaze and something inside her weakened as birdsong echoed from the treetops. At night, the whippoorwill called across the forest; in the morning, bluebirds and cardinals often fluttered from the front porch when she stepped out on her way to work. Now she knew how they felt.

Lines of weariness framed Gerard's blue eyes. Something had changed. As she waited for him to reach her, she felt a new kind of tension.

Gerard allowed himself a few seconds to feast on the sight of Megan's face. He realized in that short span how bleak the attitude at the mission had grown without her. His life too, come to think of it. The aftermath of the murder, of course, still lingered over the three-story, 25,000-square-foot building and among the employees and volunteers, but he knew the patients missed Megan's unwavering and nonjudgmental compassion, her laughter, her ability to stop a child's tears midstream with a gentle touch.

"Spending a lot of time outdoors lately?" Her voice, usually strong but gentle, with a musical lilt, strained with a transparent attempt to sound casual.

One of the first things that had attracted Gerard to Megan was her voice—since their first introduction was over the phone. The second attraction had been her straightforward honesty. She also had a sense of humor that arose at some of the most inconvenient times, but that helped her cope with the stress of her job. He even liked that about her.

He stepped onto the porch and heard that same creak of wood beneath his feet that had probably startled her earlier. "I've spent a lot of time walking and praying the past two weeks."

"On the streets, no doubt." She stepped backward as if to keep him from getting too close.

"It's where we find our patients, Megan."

"They aren't mine. Not now."

"You haven't—"

"I know, I know. I haven't fulfilled my obligation. You made that clear when I left. You think I don't know how much I owe? But it isn't going to happen in the near future, if at all, and I'm sorry, but I can't do anything about—"

"I didn't come here to argue with you."

"No?" Her gaze met his briefly, then skimmed away.

"And I didn't come here to coerce you back to Texas against your will. I have business in the area."

Her golden-brown gaze met his with a hint of disbelief. "You think a town the size of Jolly Mill has a lot of homeless?"

"I didn't say a mission. I said business."

"Oh really? You make sales calls for your own company now? Times must be hard. No one needs a lot of go-green construction pieces in this part of the country." She held her arms out. "Look around you, Gerard. No one's building anything here. We even have a few businesses that have closed."

He ignored the sarcasm in her voice. "Hans and I still need to expand."

"But here?"

"We need a location for a second manufacturing plant, and we still plan to establish the rehab center."

She blinked at him. He'd discussed his plans with her in detail, and he knew she shared his enthusiasm for those plans. He'd never told her he was considering her hometown, but hearing her talk about the community with such affection had drawn him to this place as much as her tender heart had drawn him to her.

"You don't plan to do that in Texas?" she asked.

"We're still looking, but Hans, Tess and I all feel attracted to this area for the rehab center."

"Why?"

"You've often spoken of returning here, and you make this area of the country sound appealing. There's also a depressed economy in many parts of southern Missouri, and more industry can only help. Besides, when people from the street come to rehab, we want to make sure they'll be able to make a fresh start in a fresh place with no memories of failure to haunt them."

"You can't be doing this because of me, Gerard."

"I didn't say I was. I just thought it was time I came to take a look for myself. I've done some preliminary studies, and this region could be well suited to what we want in the expansion, including people in need of a job."

"Your timing stinks. You know that, don't you? I need a chance to heal, and your being here doesn't help. Besides, we're doing well in this area financially."

He studied her features. "Your eyes are shadowed. Your skin's pale. I knew you'd suffer in silence."

She looked away.

He searched the surrounding woods for signs of another habitation, but the closest building he saw was several hundred feet away through the trees, and that appeared to be a barn.

"Probably no one's heard you screaming during your nightmares."

She shook her head.

"But you're still having them." It wasn't a question. Those screams were part of her excuse—no, make that her reason—for leaving the mission. She'd explained that her neighbors were complaining, and that her lack of sleep could put patients at risk.

Gerard felt his gaze become a touchless caress and he knew she felt it too. He couldn't help himself. After all she'd endured at the mission, until this last horrible experience, she'd been courageous and compassionate, helping all the patients she could simply because she cared. How could he not admire her?

She closed her eyes for a few seconds, and when she opened them again he saw sadness there as deep as a Texas oil well.

After losing a patient on the exam table at Christmastime from the results of a vicious poisoning by someone determined to destroy Tess, Megan had redoubled her efforts at target practice so she could better guard her patients. When with Tess, traveling or shopping, she'd carried a concealed weapon, as she had in the clinic. To lose Joni Park despite all her efforts to become a security guard as well as a physician was more than Megan could emotionally handle. Gerard continued to reproach himself since their final argument outside the mission.

His sister wasn't too happy with him either. When Tess was forced to retreat to the mission in fear of her life last year, she and Megan had formed a tight bond. Megan was the sister Tess never had, and for the past several months, Tess had hinted to Gerard that he could make that sisterly relationship legal. After some long talks with Tess these past three weeks, Gerard understood Megan so much better than he had before.

What was it about women that made it so easy for them to connect with one another and be able to read each other's minds? And why hadn't he grasped the true depth of Megan's heart sooner, without Tess's help?

"Gerard, there are barely eight hundred people living here," Megan said. "You bring Texas here and it won't be Jolly Mill anymore."

"This is strictly a fact-gathering trip. I arrived this morning and wanted to see you first."

"You drove all night."

He nodded.

"Looks like it."

"Thanks."

Something around her eyes seemed to relax. "You're seriously considering this because of what I said about Jolly Mill?"

"Have you ever known me to lie?"

She held his gaze, and a glint of the gold seemed to lighten. "Not to me because you knew I'd make you suffer if I caught you at it."

He felt his own tension settle, and he grinned at her.

"I have, however, known you to keep things from Tess," she reminded him, "when you thought you were protecting her, and there have been times when you tended to take a more paternal attitude toward me."

"You're reminding me I'm bossy?"

"Well, yeah, there's that." Her voice was heavy with sarcasm, but the corners of her lips turned up.

The two-week fight that had hovered between them over the miles had ended, just like that. Now to keep it from returning. "I couldn't let you deal with this alone," he said. "It's too big for one person to handle."

"You seem to be handling it."

"I didn't take the brunt of it. You did. And I'm not handling it alone the way you are. Tess and Sean and the whole staff know what happened. Sean and I have had some long talks about it. Who can you talk to about it?"

She looked away.

"That's what I thought," he said. "Nobody. You shouldn't be alone with the memories."

"I want to be alone."

"No, you don't."

She scowled. "You don't listen very well."

"Sometimes I have to listen to the tone of your voice instead of your words. I have to read your expression."

Megan rolled her eyes. "Gerard, I don't need to be rescued."

"Yeah. You do. And what about your patients? You're treating again, but you told me you feared for the well-being of your patients at the mission because you weren't sleeping." He reached forward and touched her cheek before she could stop him. She looked so drawn. Her skin was cold. He wanted to warm it. "You're still not getting much sleep."

"What part about my request for time didn't you understand?"

"Time to do what? Go back to the same kind of job you were doing?"

She met his gaze. "It's not the same kind of job at all. Everyone has a home and food to eat, and I don't have to cut babies out of their dead mothers. There's no comparison."

He heard the angst in her voice and he wanted to reach out and hold her in his arms and heal all her pain. Tess accused him of trying to play God, but she was wrong. "You need time from the memories, Megan, but you're not getting it, obviously. Therefore you need someone—"

"And that would be you, of course."

"Exactly."

"What would you be able to do for me?"

"Listen. Help. Support."

She shook her head. "If I talk about it, the nightmares will just get worse."

"Have they gotten any easier since you arrived here?"

She turned away, and the soft sound of her footsteps echoed across the wooden porch.

"I'll take that as a no. You wouldn't take my calls." He followed her. "Did you even read those messages Kirstie passed along? I know she gave them to you because she told me she did. In fact, she even called me back one time and apologized for you."

Megan bowed her head, and the long, ginger-colored strands of her hair glowed in the early-morning sunlight.

"That's what I thought," he said.

"Please, I'm not ready for this. I can't—"

"You're going to have to work through it because your mind isn't letting it go."

She turned, and her expression slowly hardened as her stare became a glare. "How I handle my emotional baggage is my own business."

Okay, he had that coming. Note for next time: a guy didn't just barge in on a woman before sunrise and expect a warm welcome. Why did he push so hard? Because he was right. At least this time. He knew from talking to Kirstie that Megan was struggling.

"How did you find me?" she asked.

"You left your address book behind in your apartment. Your landlord found it. You weren't answering your cell so I called every one of your friends until I reached one who didn't sound surprised when I asked about you."

She leaned against a support post beside the steps and crossed her arms. "And you felt you had a right to page through my personal property?"

"Sure did. I was worried about you when you didn't even call Tess."

"And Kirstie was willing to trust a complete stranger?" Megan asked.

"Not until I chatted with her for a while."

"Charmed her, you mean."

He grinned. "I simply convinced her I was trustworthy. You'd paved the way, of course, but she's also a good judge of character."

"She wasn't always."

"You're talking about her husband, the weakling who abandoned her after the diagnosis."

Megan's eyes widened. "She really did trust you."

He shrugged. "What can I say? I'm a trustworthy man."

Megan shoved away from the support post and gazed through the trees toward the barn Gerard had spotted earlier. There was the sadness again, not only in her eyes, but in every inch of her body, the way her shoulders slumped, the way her mouth turned down, the way she drew into herself as if trying to zip herself into a body bag.

"She told me about her blackouts," Gerard said.

"The doctor who diagnosed her called it sundowner's syndrome. How many times did you two talk?"

"Twice. I refuse to call it sundowner's until someone can prove she has chronic Alzheimer's or dementia."

"You had extended conversations, no doubt."

He nodded. "Not counting dozens of emails."

"You didn't tell her why I left the mission, did you?"

"I didn't tell her about Joni. I did give her some explanation as to why you left."

"Gerard."

"I told her you'd lost a couple of patients in the past few months but that you didn't like to talk about it. Did she mention to you that she was afraid she was being poisoned?"

Megan's expression froze into the image of a porcelain figurine, all but the eyes, which darkened with shock. "She told you that?"

"Aha! And she didn't tell you."

As if by habit, Megan smacked him gently on the arm. "Don't gloat. *Poison?* She said that word?"

"Those words exactly, and before you say anything about this to Lynley, don't. She doesn't know. Kirstie told only me."

"Why didn't she say something to me about it?"

"You refused to take her case."

"Of course I did. She needs a neurologist."

Gerard shook his head. "You still think that?"

Megan raised an elegantly arched brow. "What would you say if I told you she warned me recently that I could be in danger?"

He studied that carefully held expression. It was the one he'd seen often when Megan and Tess were playing a joke on him. Megan's emotions were all over the place this morning. "Kirstie said that?"

"I think she was talking about you. So that means you told her you were coming."

"I said I would be coming soon, but I didn't make the decision to drive here last night until she told me about the poison theory. I didn't want you to face that, along with everything else, all alone." And Kirstie had given no hint that she was suspicious of him. Quite the contrary. "She said you were in danger from me?"

A wry smile crossed Megan's lips as she slid her gaze away from him. "A certain kind of danger."

He continued to watch her, relaxing enough to enjoy yet another break from the tension. "Ah. I see." He couldn't help returning the smile, and he did it in double quantity, though Megan still avoided his gaze. "She's a perceptive lady. You've spoken to her of us then." He knew she had. Kirstie had alluded to hearing his name mentioned quite a few times over the past year or so.

"Of you. Singular."

He could tell by the light in Megan's eyes that she was also enjoying the break in tension, temporary though it may be. "Well, that's still good. She said you told her how strong I was, that I was an ex-cop."

"Did you tell her you forced me to take classes to get a license to carry—"

"I did not force you to do that."

Megan blinked up at him. "I hope you didn't lie to her. She can see through lies these days, and she does not take kindly to them."

"I didn't force you to get the license. I strongly suggested it because of the section of town where we're located."

"You threatened me with my life."

"I did not. I only suggested you might save a life in more ways than—"

He realized too late that he should have let it drop when Megan turned away, shoulders once again drooping, eyes closing in pain.

"Kirstie did share your description of me," he said, gently resting a hand on her back. "Even I was impressed. I'm a tough, giant blond guy with strikingly beautiful blue eyes, and no woman should be able to resist me."

Megan turned back. "I did *not* say that."

Gerard chuckled. "No, wait. You said I was still a tough cop at heart."

"Something like that."

"Kirstie did agree with you that I tend to growl on occasion."

"Well, here we are on your favorite subject again," Megan drawled in the Texas twang she'd developed during her time in the town of Southern heat. "You."

"Ouch."

He watched the pain ease from around Megan's eyes again as the discussion lightened. Something inside her was sealed up like a brand-new Deepfreeze. Maybe she truly couldn't have this conversation with him yet. This argument. This call to return to the scene of the crime and work through the tangle of confusion and pain that left them both with open wounds.

She was needed here now, for Kirstie and Lynley. She finally realized she could help Kirstie. Though she didn't realize it yet, Gerard too, needed to be here. In time, they'd get through the tangle and set things right again.

THREE

Megan studied Gerard's profile as he gazed out into the forest. She was caught once again in the gale-force wind that was Gerard Vance, and she felt a desperate need to tell him everything that had happened since they'd last talked. Really talked. As in, sharing their thoughts, debating their gut feelings, even touching souls on occasion.

She'd missed that so much since the world flew apart. Now there was this huge black hole in the universe keeping her from Gerard and Tess and all her friends at the mission, because she couldn't get past what happened and reconnect with them. She didn't even have time, right now, to find her way back to sanity here in Jolly Mill because of Kirstie.

"Poison," she said, drawing Gerard's gaze back to her. "Drugging of some kind. Do you really think it's possible? Here in Jolly Mill?" Megan felt the strength of Gerard's presence encompass the wooden front porch, the yard, possibly even threaten to charm the fluttering and chirping birds from the trees.

"There's evil everywhere," he said. "Even here in paradise."

"When did you first talk to Kirstie?"

"A week and a half ago. I thought I'd give you a little

more time, warn you I'd be coming here so you wouldn't be caught off guard. I left messages for you with Kirstie, and she, of course, recognized my name."

The teasing lilt in his voice brought a surprising sting of tears to Megan's eyes. She swallowed. So much had been lost. Not only had that heinous killer destroyed the life of a very pregnant young woman, but he'd destroyed a powerful relationship between two people falling in love... hadn't he?

"So of course," Megan said, swallowing again, "charming as Kirstie is, she drew you out, got more information from you about yourself."

"About us, I think. That's why she warned you of danger." Still that hint of a tease in his voice. "Once I told her about how much we valued you at the clinic, she opened up and started to talk about your friendship with Lynley and how much you meant to her."

Megan narrowed her eyes at him. "Don't start me on any guilt trips."

"How's that?"

"She wants me to take her case. She doesn't believe she has Alzheimer's."

"Neither do you," Gerard said.

Megan held his gaze. How did he read her mind so well? "I referred her to two of the best specialists in the region, and she didn't want to go to them. She wants me or no one, but she never said a word to me about her suspicions of poison."

"She knows you've been through some kind of trauma, and she's willing to sacrifice her own health in order to walk on eggshells around you, keep you from being stressed."

Megan was amazed by how easily she was suddenly coming to tears this morning. "I'm not a specialist."

"But you are." Gerard's footsteps echoed across the porch as he drew closer to Megan. "You specialize in people. As you've told me more than once when treating patients at the mission, Alzheimer's can be a trash-can diagnosis, and people with mental problems aren't trash."

Megan winced. He was using her words against her. "Speaking of Kirstie, I got a call about her before you so rudely arrived at my door before daybreak." She glanced at her watch, then reached into her bag to check her cell phone. Either Lynley hadn't tried to call or she was in an area without coverage and couldn't call. "She's missing."

"Again?"

Megan nodded. She took a deep breath, and it wasn't until that breath came back out as steam in the air that she suddenly realized it was chilly. She brushed by Gerard and went down the steps. "I told Lynley I'd check Kirstie out at the clinic."

"I'll come with you."

Megan couldn't resist a glance back up at Gerard, the firm jawline with an overnight shadow, the sudden cloud of worry in his blue eyes.

What was it about the man that made her feel stronger? Why did she suddenly feel capable of doing whatever she needed to for Kirstie? He gave her strength, and she had longed for that strength these past two weeks—had longed for it so much that she'd even tried to resort to prayer a couple of times. Gerard Vance reflected the strength of the God he served when he wasn't coming across as the ultimate bossy alpha male.

"If you come with me, the whole town will be talking," she said.

"Let 'em talk."

"Easy for you to say. You don't have to live here."

"Then I'll drive myself and help search."

Megan scowled at him. "You don't know what she looks like."

"Actually, I do. Hazel eyes, heart-shaped face, dimples, wavy blond hair. It is the computer age, you know."

Megan pushed past a hibiscus as tall as she was. Droplets of dew sprinkled across her face. "We have plenty of people in town who know her and know where to look."

"No one knows exactly where to look right now or she'd have been found." Gerard fell into step beside her.

She brushed past moisture-drenched evergreen shrubs to keep from feeling the warmth of him beside her. She'd be dripping by the time she reached the clinic at this rate. But hadn't she known she would react this way to his presence? It was why she hadn't returned his calls. Yet how was she supposed to tell him that? Say, "Sorry, Gerard, but I can't have you around because when you're near me I can't think straight"?

"You didn't take enough time for closure so you're avoiding me," he said.

"I don't need closure. I need time to reverse about three weeks."

"So do I, but that's not going to happen. I have to deal with today just as it is. So do you."

"I can only deal with one thing at a time."

"Understood. We'll focus on Kirstie, but first, would you tell me why I didn't receive a request for a reference from your new employer?"

Megan gritted her teeth and her footsteps slowed. She saw the glint of steel in Gerard's gaze and braced herself for yet more arguing. Sometimes she felt there was nothing he liked better.

Gerard bit back a grin as he watched Megan's eyes flash. By now Tess would've blown sky-high at his goading. Megan took a lot more from him.

"Alec didn't need a reference." Megan's words were measured, her voice a little lower than usual. "We've known each other since kindergarten. This cottage belongs to his family."

Now they were getting somewhere. Gerard didn't like it, but at least it was out in the open. "Of course. Small town, no one's a stranger. Alec Thompson's his name, right?"

She pushed aside a branch of a juniper tree and allowed it to slap back into his face. "Don't you dare tell me you called him about me too."

"Nope, I just studied him."

She turned a scowl on Gerard, then stepped ahead of him and continued toward her car. "How?"

"Internet. You really should try it sometime."

"You're not really a cop anymore, you know."

"Megan, I didn't gather the information to hurt the man."

"So why were you checking him out?"

"The more a person knows, the better his chances of getting a job done."

She stopped and turned so quickly he almost stumbled over her. "What job?"

"I have to be able to trust the people I work with. I may not be a cop any longer, but I'm still responsible for the safety of a lot of people who don't have anyplace else to go. Unlike you, I can't just quit my job and leave."

Her grimace told him his words had plunged deeply enough to draw blood. Maybe she'd take the bait.

"You're right." Her gold-bronze eyes flashed a few sparks of lightning. "I'm nothing like you. Get used to it. I failed, okay?"

He held up a finger. "First of all, I checked Alec Thompson because it's helpful for me to know that there's been a layoff at the casket factory owned by the Thompson family, thus the need for new jobs in the area. Knowing that his father apparently abandoned the family and disappeared from the face of the earth when Alec was in high school tells me more about Alec and the Thompson businesses."

"Why do you need to know that?"

"I need to know who handles the businesses and has the goodwill of the people." Gerard held up a second finger. "It's also nice to get to know the kind of people I might be working with, even hiring, if it comes to that, and knowing the kind of employees hired by the company will help with that." Three fingers. "Medical care and supportive services, and room for expansion, are vital. I have my work cut out for me if this is where I plan to set up shop."

Some of the fire left her eyes. Megan was always one to see reason, and though she could get cranky and had a sharp tongue when her patients were in danger, she wasn't one to hold a grudge over the small things. "The casket factory did have a big layoff," she mused. "I heard it around town."

"But not from Alec? He didn't tell you how hard the economy was hitting his pocketbook?" Gerard found it difficult to keep a thread of satisfaction from his voice. Jealousy didn't become him. Not that he cared.

Alec Thompson had a clean record, had served four years total in the navy and was legally married, but since his wife had lived in California for at least the past year, he was likely living alone. Amazing how public a person's life became online these days. The man was a handsome devil too, according to Gerard's sister. Tess had discerning tastes, but the term *devil* had appealed more to Gerard.

"I read that he also runs the grocery in town," Gerard said.

"His family owns it but he doesn't manage it," Megan

said. "So I guess you can't believe everything you find online, can you?" she taunted. "He took over the family businesses his parents established twenty-five years ago." Megan opened her car door then turned to look up at Gerard. "His mother is an astute businesswoman, and the clinic was her idea. They're nice people, Gerard."

"I have no doubt of that."

"They aren't overworking me and I'm being well-reimbursed. Nora's letting me stay at the cottage for free. Thanks to their generosity, I may be able to pay off my school loans, after all. You'll like her. You'll also like Alec, whether you want to or not."

Tess might. Gerard definitely did not. "I will meet him, I'm sure."

Megan slid behind the steering wheel of her Neo, but when she reached to close the door, he caught it.

"You're out here in the middle of nowhere," he said. "You wanted to be as far from the city as you could get—even as far from Jolly Mill as you could get."

"I like the country. I always have." She started the car. The engine still had that slight rattle Gerard had intended to fix for her.

He didn't release the door. "What you're doing isn't healthy, Megan."

"What I'm doing is helping a friend." She gave him a pointed look then jerked her head toward the hand that held the door. "Do you mind?"

He didn't move. "One of the reasons I kept trying to reach you was because tuberculosis has been making a recurrence on the street, and you worked closely with many patients."

"Yet you didn't tell Kirstie about that, or call my new boss?"

"I didn't want another person to do my job for me."

"I'm not your job."

The tip of Gerard's tongue scrubbed at his teeth. "It's my job to see to the welfare of my employees, and you were my employee when you worked with the patients at the clinic."

"I get my yearly TB test, I don't have night sweats, unexplained weight loss or a dry cough—"

"You do need more time off."

"Make up your mind. A few minutes ago you wanted me to be Kirstie's physician."

"One patient. That's nothing like going back to work at a busy clinic."

Megan put her hands on the steering wheel. "This isn't helping."

"I'm sorry."

Megan's cell phone rang, and she stiffened. Gerard could tell she hadn't calmed down as well as she wanted to pretend she had. She took a breath and reached for the cell.

Gerard watched her expression as she took the call. Instant relief.

"They found Kirstie?" he asked.

Megan irritably motioned for him to shut up. He knew that gesture. She'd used it enough times at the mission.

"We'll have to check to see if she inhaled any creek water," Megan said. "Just get her to the clinic and I'll meet you there." She flipped the cell shut and reached for the door. "I have to go to Kirstie."

"I'll follow you there."

"Gerard, they've found her, and you don't need to be at the clinic."

"It's time I started meeting some of the people, checking out the town. You're a big girl, you can handle a few rumors, can't you?"

With a sigh, Megan started the engine and gunned it. "Fine, if you can keep up, but I warn you, I drive the way I always have."

Gerard chuckled as he watched her burn a doughnut in the leaves and grass and miss his car by half a foot. Had it not occurred to her that he'd already studied the layout of Jolly Mill? He would take his time and enjoy the drive now that he knew Kirstie had been found.

FOUR

Kirstie Marshal no longer held out hope of regaining her dignity anytime soon, especially not in Jolly Mill. She had mud up her nose, silt between her teeth and fish eggs in her hair. When she caught a reflection of herself in the glass entryway to the clinic, a leaf appeared to be sticking out of her right ear—or was that part of her hair? If Lynley's hands weren't already trembling so badly she'd barely been able to steer the car to the clinic, Kirstie would have goosed her.

"I can't believe you'd allow me to appear in public like this," she muttered, fighting Lynley's attempts to hold on to her arm from the car to the clinic.

"I want to make sure you're okay."

Kirstie pulled away long enough to tug the leaf from her hair. "I'm fine except for the public humiliation."

"And bloody feet." Lynley's serious coal-brown eyes, lustrous from recent tears, narrowed slightly. She blinked as if seeing her mother's face for the first time. Her hair, dark as twilight, the way Kirstie's once was, stood out in odd directions, proving she'd plunged from bedclothes to search clothes without a glance in the mirror. No toothbrush had touched those pretty white teeth this morning, that was for sure.

"How did you discover I was gone?" Kirstie didn't want her kid doing bed checks at thirty-minute intervals.

"Your bedroom door was open and the light was still on. The light woke me up."

"You fell asleep studying again?"

Lynley nodded. "You sleep with the door closed, not to mention the lights out."

Kirstie sighed. "Sorry again, sweetie. You're not old enough to be part of the sandwich generation. You don't even have kids. And I'm not an old moldy piece of bread."

"No, you're not, so stop expecting me to throw you away like one."

"That isn't what I'm doing."

Carmen Delaney, clinic director and a stalwart member of Kirstie's shrinking band of trusted friends, opened the inner door and held it for them, keys still jingling in her hands. She had her silvery-blond hair pulled straight back from her face in a severe ponytail.

Carmen was the only forty-eight-year-old Kirstie knew who had a face pretty enough—and taut enough—to support such severity. Kirstie knew, however, that Carmen kept that rubber band tight to smooth out the lines that had begun to form. Soon she'd be bald, what with the bleaching and the tugging. Then what would she use to keep those wrinkles stretched?

Oh, that's right, menopause time. Soon the fat will fill those wrinkled places quite nicely. Poor Carmen was in for the shock of her life anytime now, if she hadn't already learned something from Kirstie's and Nora's shared experiences.

"Kirstie, honey, you gave us all a scare and a half!" Carmen said. "Lynley, how's she doing?"

"I can answer that question for myself, thank you very much." Kirstie limped, barefoot and still dripping leaves and mud, onto the smooth wooden floor of the waiting room. "I'm not elderly yet. I can swim, apparently, even when I'm out of my mind."

"You mean you found a place along Capps Creek deep enough for swimming in this drought?" Carmen asked.

"I found her at the edge of the mill pond," Lynley said.

Kirstie held her arms out and looked at the mud. "Don't ask me how it happened. I came to myself up on a cliff somewhere just before the ground gave way."

"Did you get hurt?" Carmen asked.

"No. I'm fine. It's just a little blood."

"We'll find out as soon as we get her into the exam room," Lynley said. "I expect Megan'll come racing up any moment."

"Why bother Megan for a few cuts and bruises?" Kirstie said the words, feeling like a fraud. She wanted Megan here more than Lynley did, though at the same time, she hesitated to consider dragging Megan into this mess more deeply than she already was. Something was going on with her, and she didn't seem able to talk about it to her closest friends. Although Megan was one of the strongest and most resilient young women Kirstie had ever known, this kind of pressure might overwhelm even her.

"I could just wander back to an exam room and take a look at these feet myself," Kirstie said. "Then I can walk home if someone will loan me some shoes." She knew that would never go over, even if it was only a few blocks away. "Then you can all get to work on the real patients."

"No real patients for an hour," Carmen said. "Megan won't want you walking home. She may even decide to keep you here for observation."

Kirstie grunted. Not if her plan panned out. Of course, in order for that to happen, one had to remain in one's right mind.

"She'll need to see if you inhaled any of that creek water," Carmen said.

"More likely silt." Lynley's voice continued to tremble.

"Oh, sweetie," Carmen said, wrapping an arm around Lynley—something Kirstie should've done. "She's going to be just fine. This may be just what we need to convince Megan to run some tests of her own."

"She turned us down, remember?"

Kirstie hated that tremor in her daughter's voice. "She had her reasons, sweetie."

"What reason could she possibly have had to turn down—"

"None of our business what the reason is." Kirstie met Carmen's gaze of understanding, then patted Lynley's cold, moist cheek. "But I expect it has something to do with wanting me in more experienced hands. You want someone placing their whole life, their future, all their hopes in your hands when you aren't a specialist in the field? You want to be responsible for that kind of burden?"

"But you're not going to either of the other specialists." Lynley's voice no longer trembled, but there was a hint of rancor in place of the agitation.

It seemed that ever since Lynley arrived back in Jolly Mill, her emotions had swung from fear to anger to grief. She didn't know how obvious it was to everyone that she had begun the grieving process. Kirstie wished she could swallow all that pain for her precious daughter, but her own emotions kept getting in the way.

"Don't tell me you're blaming Megan for that," Carmen said. "Honey, if you ask me, our Megan's barely hanging on as it is. Did you see her face when she caught sight of Forrest the other day?"

"Who?"

"You know, as in Gump. The man with the wild gray hair who walks all over the place."

"You're talking about Kendall Ross," Lynley said. "He looks like a homeless man, but he has a house and three kids and a wife."

"I know, plus he has three cats and two dogs, but he looks homeless. Smells it too, sometimes, and he talks to himself."

"So do I," Kirstie muttered.

"Recovering addict, you know," Carmen said. "Last I heard he was under house arrest."

Kirstie fingered her mud-stiff hair.

"Anyway, Megan's face went white as my refrigerator when he walked past the clinic a couple of days ago," Carmen continued as if she hadn't been interrupted. "That long, bushy, gray hair of his was flying every which way. Megan's eyes teared up and she had to get to the bathroom quick. If you ask me, our poor Megan worked with the homeless a little too long and her heart just broke. She's burned out at the age of thirty-two."

"Wish she wasn't living alone," Kirstie said.

"I told her she could stay in my guest room," Carmen said. "And Nora has that whole huge house to herself and begged Megan to move in with her and keep her company. Nothing doing. The best she could do was give Megan that isolated cabin in the woods."

"Megan always did love that place," Lynley said. "She has what she wants."

Kirstie glanced out the window and saw a bright yellow car flashing through the shadows of trees overhanging the road. Hmm. Maybe this wasn't such a bad situation, after all. Quite a way behind the yellow Neo came another car, bright red, and Kirstie suppressed a smile. If she wasn't mistaken, the cavalry had arrived. *Thank you, Jesus!*

"She'll have to at least weigh in on your case now, won't she?" Carmen asked, voicing Kirstie's thoughts as she stepped up beside her at the window.

"Nope. Let's lie low for a bit, okay? She doesn't need that right now." *Such a hypocrite, Kirstie.*

Carmen gave Kirstie a once-over. "Wouldn't hurt you to get some street clothes on."

"She's not walking home, anyway," Lynley said. "I'll drive her."

Kirstie looked down at her mud-caked nightgown. "I've decided to make a new fashion statement. I call it 'Blackout Chic.' I might as well capitalize on all the attention my loving daughter keeps sending my way."

"Mom," Lynley warned. "You want me to just let you wander out in the forest like a wild animal?"

"Wild animals should be caged to protect themselves." Kirstie sucked on her tongue to corral further hurtful words.

"I can't believe you said that." Tears once more filled Lynley's eyes.

"Girls," Carmen said, "you could both use a little color, a little foundation, some eye-popping makeup. Want to borrow mine for the day?"

They ignored her, as she obviously expected them to, but she opened a case of her own wares at any rate and pulled out a tube of concealer. "At least prepare for patients. You can't have them thinking someone died on the table this morning."

Kirstie sighed. Perhaps insulating Lynley from so many of life's trials when she was a child had hindered her emotional growth; she could still be easily wounded, at least by her mother's sarcasm. She'd always been tenderhearted. With no siblings to be supportive of her—or to teach her how to better integrate—she had needed the extra attention, especially since she had a father who preferred reinforcing his delusions of manhood with as many women as he could unearth, rob from the cradle or lure away from other men.

Right now, Lynley was still too fragile after her divorce from Barry's clone. Girls really did marry their daddies.

"Megan should be here any second. I hope she at least had time to put her face on," Carmen said. "And it's possible you'll have the chance to convince Megan to give us another opinion. She's a good diagnostician."

"And as she's said," Kirstie reminded her friend, "she's too close to the case herself. Of course, if she were to diagnose me with Alzheimer's also, then maybe Lynley would give up and let me be placed in a lock-down unit and stop wasting her nights chasing after me." Kirstie's feet hurt, and this hard wooden floor didn't help matters.

Lynley glanced at Carmen and then glared at Kirstie. "There's that word again. Wasting? Really. You're my mother."

"You can't watch me every second. You'll ruin your own future."

"It usually happens at night. We could set up an alarm—"

"No!" Kirstie took a slow breath. "What kind of mother would I be if I allowed you to give up your life for mine?"

"It's not over yet. We'll figure something out. And don't even think about getting Megan to help you gang up on me again. She tried to this morning, you know. No nursing facility. Period."

Carmen waved an arm between the two of them. "Excuse me? Would you two postpone this boxing match until I'm out of hearing range? And speaking of our doctor…" She gestured toward the parking lot, where

Megan pulled in with her bright, eye-hurting Neo, followed closely by a red mini SUV. With a man inside.

Kirstie smiled. Wow. Was she finally going to meet, face-to-face, the unacknowledged man in her darling Megan's life? He was some man. Not Megan's type at all. Megan had always been attracted to the soft-spoken intellectual. This time, however, she might need to bend a little.

Megan jerked her car to a stop, had the door open less than a second later, and was hot-footing it toward the front door as she shoved her keys into her oversize purse.

She didn't spare a glance for her stalker. She wasn't wearing her usual scrubs and lab coat.

"That must be him," Kirstie murmured.

"Who?" Carmen's green eyes widened as the man got out of his car and stood up. "Wow."

Kirstie smiled. The sun appeared to dazzle his face— but that could have been because his face was so close to the sun.

Kirstie reached for a tissue and blew her nose. "And here I am looking and smelling like a bed of dried fish eggs. Oh my goodness, he's a hunk. Would you look at him?"

"Who is he?" Oh yeah, Carmen could be smitten. Six years was too much time to grieve even the best of men, and though Gil had been a better man than Barry, his idea of a romantic gesture had been taking out the trash every couple of weeks. Lack of exercise was why he'd succumbed early in life to a premature heart attack.

"Careful, Carmen," Kirstie said. "He's too young for either of us. I could be wrong, but I'm pretty sure he's Megan's boss."

"Alec Thompson is Megan's boss," Lynley said.

"I mean her boss in Corpus Christi."

Carmen leaned closer to the window for a better look, and a bemused smile tipped her curvy pink lips. "That guy she couldn't shut up about the day she flew up here for Lynley's divorce party?"

"It wasn't a party," Lynley said. "It was commiseration."

For Kirstie, it had been a party. "He fits her description, doesn't he?"

"He still runs the rescue mission?" Carmen asked.

"He also matches the hunky photo his sister took for his online profile."

Lynley cleared her throat as if to remind them she was still in the room. "Would you please stop talking about hunky men in front of your only child?"

Kirstie bit her tongue and pressed her lips together. So it was fine for Barry to play all over any field he wished, but it wasn't okay for Barry's long-suffering wife, even after he'd abandoned her? Did Lynley think her mother was going to welcome her father back with open arms after that final slap in the face?

"I don't think he's right for Megan. She hasn't wanted to talk about him," Lynley said at last, wavering from her mother's stare.

"Why not?" Carmen asked. "She used to talk about him all the time. If that's him."

Kirstie cast another glance out the window and gave a small sigh. Oh, it was him, all right.

"Things change," Lynley said.

Kirstie wished desperately for a mirror. "Don't be silly, honey. Are we supposed to ignore his presence when he walks through the door so Megan's feelings won't be hurt? You think she's that fragile?"

"Why should he even come through the door?" Lynley

asked. "Why is he here? She doesn't work for him now and she obviously doesn't want him here."

"She may still be employed by him," Kirstie said. "In fact, even if she isn't, I believe he has as much right to be here as any other businessman interested in expanding his enterprise."

The door flew open and Megan entered so quickly it seemed she stirred up a breeze, but Kirstie's announcement had attracted all the attention for the moment.

The looks of confusion Carmen and Lynley gave Kirstie at her news were almost worth the morning's disappointments and painful feet.

"Honey," Kirstie greeted Megan, "if you don't grab that man, I will."

Megan gave Kirstie a once-over. "I see you're in fighting form," she said as she continued past them. "Let me check you out. Is that blood on the floor? Come on back here, Kirstie."

"Okay, maybe I won't grab him," Kirstie said as she hobbled toward the first exam room, where Megan had retreated, "but you can bet Carmen will. He's what, thirty-six? Thirty-eight?"

"Thirty-five."

"Still no problem. Thirteen years is hardly an age difference these days."

Lynley attempted to catch her mother's arm.

Kirstie pulled away. "Stay out here and make Mr. Vance comfortable. Tell him I'm going to be fine."

"What does it matter to him?"

"I believe it does, honey. I've spoken with him a couple of times on the phone, and remember what he does for his life's work. He cares for others. Just like we do. Just like Megan does. Be nice."

"I want to go in with you," Lynley said.

"I want doctor-patient confidentiality." Kirstie glanced once more out the window and grinned at the retro tie-dyed T-shirt the man filled out so well. "Talk to the hunk."

"But what's he doing here at the clinic?"

"Don't ask me, ask him. Remember, no flirting, Lynley. He may be taken." Kirstie gave Carmen a glare. "That goes for you too."

"No promises. I've got dibs if Megan dumps him."

Suppressing a chuckle of satisfaction, Kirstie followed Megan into the exam room. When she could find her brain, she was still a force to be reckoned with.

While Megan rushed across the parking lot and into the clinic, Gerard took his time and scoped out the idyllic Jolly Mill setting. The scent of Capps Creek was a little fishier than it ordinarily would be, he knew, because of recent drought.

The gray brick clinic had white shutters and interesting gingerbread trim at the roof's edge. It helped the building blend in with the colorful Victorian style of surrounding shops and houses. It was pretty much what he'd expected from Megan's description, though perhaps a little more polished than she'd mentioned.

He didn't take Megan's snub personally as she disappeared into the bowels of the clinic with the lady he recognized as Kirstie. He had second-guessed his decision to follow Megan to the clinic but not seriously enough to actually change his mind. He knew his presence here would be hard on her, but he wanted to make sure Kirstie was okay. He didn't wish to embarrass Megan by drawing attention to their friendship, but he was going to be here awhile if things worked out right. And he planned to see to it that they did work out right.

He also wanted to meet her friends and check out

the competition, and he wanted her to get accustomed to seeing him in other settings besides the mission. That was what courtship was all about, and though she didn't realize it, Gerard had no doubt about his intentions.

As for Kirstie, he needed to be sure she was okay because he already felt a kinship to her. Probably everyone else did too. She reminded him of Megan. A person couldn't miss the kindness in her voice.

He studied the outside of the clinic as he reached for the exterior door. Someone had attached security cameras to the outer corners of the building, and when he stepped through the interior entrance he noticed two more. Someone had money to spare, but who thought it necessary to install security in Jolly Mill? Maybe he would need to check out some of the risks before he made any decisions about future plans in this location.

Two women stood talking softly in the middle of the waiting room when he entered. The older woman with interesting green eyes and a blond ponytail stepped forward with a smile. "You must be Mr. Vance, of the Vance Rescue Mission." She had the drawl of someone from much farther south.

"Yes, ma'am. You can call me Gerard."

"Your reputation precedes you." She held out her hand. "I'm Carmen Delaney, a longtime friend of Megan's, and of Kirstie's…and of pretty much everyone else in Jolly Mill."

He took the proffered hand. "I know Megan's a good friend to have. I believe Kirstie is too."

Carmen nodded, casting a quick glance toward the other, younger woman with the dark mess of hair and dark eyes who stood staring at him. "Megan's always spoken highly of you. To hear her tell it, you're Mother Teresa in a very nice—" she paused and gave him a once-over "—excellent male form."

He smiled and focused on not blushing, then studied the younger woman with the curious gaze. The troubled gaze. If this was who he suspected her to be, Megan was keeping her secrets and so was Kirstie. And the young woman probably felt she had good reason to distrust any male right now since, according to Kirstie, she'd been betrayed by the two most important men in her life.

"I came to make sure Kirstie's okay," he said. "I was with Megan when she received the call this morning."

Two pairs of eyes widened, and he realized Megan had good reason to avoid him. He did not have the grace and poise of his sister, or even his brother, for that matter. The call had come at six—not a time one typically entertained polite company.

"I arrived here from Texas early this morning," he explained, silently commanding the heat to avoid his face. "When Megan worked for me at the mission, she had a reputation for arising before dawn to study for an hour before coming to work. I hadn't realized she'd changed her habits." He gestured to the brown-red splotches on the floor. "Is Kirstie okay?"

"For someone who ran barefoot through the woods last night and took a swim with the trout this morning, I'd say she's holding up pretty well," Carmen told him, then gestured to the dark-haired younger woman. "We call the mannequin Lynley."

The woman beside her blinked then gave Carmen a frown. "I'm Kirstie's daughter," Lynley told him, not bothering to offer him her hand or even a smile.

"And Megan's best friend since babyhood, according to Megan," Gerard said.

"You'll have to excuse her," Carmen told him. "It's a

little early in the day for her to make small talk with an Adonis."

Lynley shot Carmen a hot look. "Sorry. It's been a long night. Carmen was just getting ready to make some coffee." She gave the blonde another look. "Weren't you?"

Carmen held the look for a long, rebellious moment, but she finally excused herself with another quick and extremely friendly smile at Gerard.

He grinned. There were times when he wouldn't mind gaining a few years. He'd found that many women past forty had worked through some snags of deceit and vanity of earlier adulthood, and had learned to express themselves with more honesty.

He'd found it invigorating that Megan didn't have a problem with vanity, which was a good thing because her professional ability and intelligence were always going to be challenged by the impact of her beauty, no matter how old she got.

She didn't typically practice deceit either. The major deceit she was practicing right now was on herself. That disturbed him.

Lynley sank into the closest chair with a quiet sigh and a slight aroma of fish. A little less statuesque than Megan, she had an economy of movement that fit a good nurse like a second skin and an air of serious worry that never helped a thing.

"My mother seems to know a whole lot more about you than I do." Lynley's voice held a curious mixture of suspicion and envy, and there was a slight lilt to her words that resembled Kirstie's warm vocal mannerisms. "She mentioned talking to you, but I didn't know you were actually coming here."

"For a talkative woman it sounds as if Kirstie can keep

her own counsel when she wants to." He gestured to the bloodstains on the floor. "Were the wounds bad?"

"They'll heal quickly if she'll just stay off her feet for a while. That won't happen. Do you mind telling me how you know my mother so well?"

"I reached her by phone when I was searching for Megan."

"Did it occur to you that if Megan had wanted you to find her she'd have told you where she was?"

Gerard nodded with approval. She was loyal to her friends. "The relationship between Megan and me is strictly between Megan and me."

"What happened in Corpus Christi?"

Not for the first time, he was glad the whole story hadn't been released to the press, and he was still fighting to keep the specifics from the public. Megan didn't need the additional grief, and the rescue mission didn't need the notoriety.

"A couple of killers have slipped past our sentinels in recent months," he told Lynley.

"And?"

"Working in a mission clinic can be a dangerous job. Did she tell you about it?"

Lynley looked away, shook her head, glanced up toward one of the cameras.

"We've beefed up our guard," he assured Lynley.

"She'll never go back."

Gerard felt stiffening in his chest. Her words resonated with assurance. He suspected she might know what she was talking about. But things could change.

For instance, his presence here wasn't simply meant to satisfy his curiosity—nor was he here to satisfy the curiosity of Megan's friends. He was a more intentional man than that. But several times he had questioned himself on the drive: Was he serious about planning a future here when the woman he loved didn't even seem to want him in Jolly Mill?

"So you're an ex-cop," Lynley said quietly, studying him.

He nodded.

"You know about my mother, obviously. Has she told you she's been misdiagnosed?"

He held Lynley's gaze for a moment then nodded.

She looked away, and moisture filmed her eyes. "I just finished dragging her out of the mill pond. She could've drowned. She needs help, Mr. Vance, and no one seems interested in giving it to her, not even Megan."

"Haven't you always been able to trust Megan?" he asked.

Lynley met his gaze.

"Hasn't she always been there for you?"

She hesitated before nodding. "But people change."

"You're absolutely right. People either grow and mature from the impact of life's punches or they grow sour and old before their time. I can tell you for a fact that Megan's one of the good ones, no matter what your experiences have been with other people in your life."

Before Lynley could question him or reply, Carmen returned from the back room. "Coffee's brewing and your tea is steeping, Mistress Lynley," she said with an overdone curtsy. "Nora said she was baking a fresh batch of cookies today, and Mr. Vance, you do not want to miss that treat."

"Call me Gerard," he said as he stood.

"Wow, and a real gentleman." Carmen sank into the deep cushion of the chair beside him. "Why don't you tell us a little about yourself?"

He grinned as he ventured to his chair. Exactly what he'd hoped for—a chance to get acquainted with Megan's friends, and Kirstie's. Now...where to start...

FIVE

Megan was jotting down vitals when she heard a watery sniff. She glanced toward the exam bed to find a tear caressing a clean portion of Kirstie's smooth porcelain cheek with the trajectory of a falling star. It splattered on the thick fold of the blanket Megan had tucked around Kirstie after checking her over and treating her cut and bruised feet.

"Still hurting?"

Kirstie shook her head. "I'm fine."

"Sure you are. You act fine." Every vital number so far was within normal parameters, except the blood pressure was slightly elevated because of the pain.

"I want you to draw blood," Kirstie said. "I think I may be getting poisoned."

There, the subject had been brought up at last. Megan's patience rewarded. Another tear trickled down Kirstie's face. In that moment, she seemed younger than Megan by twenty years, not older. The chin-length curls of her blond hair nearly blended with the paleness of her skin. The hazel eyes, barely touched by evidence of the lines of laughter that had always been part of Kirstie's life, seemed to have had their color depleted by the tears.

"Gerard mentioned that this morning," Megan said.

"Good. He saved me some time explaining." The normally warm tones of Kirstie's voice sounded fragile, so unlike the way she'd sounded out in the waiting room moments ago. That was Kirstie, always strong for her daughter.

"I know I've asked you about this before, but is Dr. Kelsey positive that none of the chemo drugs would have had an effect on your memory? I can call him for a consultation."

"The chemo ended two years ago," Kirstie said.

"Delayed reaction, perhaps?" Megan asked. "The results of the initial trials may have a bearing—"

"They showed no kind of mental lapse side effects." The misty green-gold of Kirstie's eyes seemed to soften further as she looked up at Megan at last. "But thanks for asking over and over and over."

"I'm not finished asking." Megan sat down on the exam stool. "When Gerard mentioned poisoning—"

"I know, you thought about a possible metastasis to the brain or reaction to the chemo. We've talked about it. I have become adept at online searches."

"I have access to physician sites, and I found nothing. I started the search as soon as I heard about the blackouts. You know this."

"That's why I think it's time to try finding some other source of poison," Kirstie said. "And by that I mean intentional."

Megan closed her eyes as the words hovered. The prospects could be the beginning of yet another nightmare. She was in the eye of some kind of storm, and she could not escape. There seemed to be a killer or a wannabe murderer on every street corner.

"I know that nothing's shown on any of my previous blood tests," Kirstie said. "You and Lynley are the only ones willing to consider other options besides that awful *A*-word."

"And Gerard."

"Oh, bless that gorgeous man."

"And Carmen."

"Loyal to the end."

"And Nora."

Kirstie gave her a faint smile. "You've made your point. Yes, I have friends, but none of my other friends can help me the way you can, and none are so indomitable."

"Oh really? You think Carmen's a weakling? Nora?"

"I'm just saying, it feels to me that to the medical world I'm a middle-aged crazy woman who should be locked away."

"I thought you wanted to be locked away."

"I want to be kept safe until we find out what's going on so things like this," Kirstie said, holding up her feet, "don't happen again."

"I'll need copies of all your medical files," Megan said.

"You mean you're actually taking on my case?"

"Not that I'm sure I can do a lot of good, but we can at least get started."

Lines of anxiety touched the corners of Kirstie's lips. "You mean that? You're a smart woman, but you're not going to find anything in those records the other doctor wouldn't have found. I want a new series of tests."

"I know. For poisons. But you know how hit-and-miss that's going to be. It won't hurt for me to study your medical file. Maybe I'll find something there that's been overlooked."

Kirstie's lids lowered. One more crystalline droplet escaped her eye.

In the thirty-two years Megan had known Kirstie, only twice had the life-loving, bubbly woman been caught crying in public. The first time was the day Lynley married Dodge Knowles. Megan suspected at the time that those tears of supposed joy were liberally mixed with sadness—not because Kirstie was one of those clingy mothers who resented anyone else in her child's life, but because she had little faith in Lynley's judgment when it came to men.

Kirstie had learned the hard way how to distinguish an honest man from a scoundrel, whereas Lynley still carried hope that her own father might one day turn out to be a good man after all.

The second time Kirstie cried in front of others was the day Dodge divorced Lynley, and she saw the heartbreak she had suspected, from the day of the wedding, that her daughter would endure.

Megan believed those tears of supposed sadness—though not touched by outright joy—may have been relief. Having one's daughter dumped by one's son-in-law for another woman was infuriating, of course. After watching that daughter suffer, however, through four years of a verbally abusive marriage with a self-righteous, strutting rooster who used God's name and carefully edited verses from the Bible to emotionally beat Lynley into submission, the legal ending of the nightmare was a relief for all.

Megan had flown from Corpus Christi to celebrate with Lynley, Kirstie, Carmen and Nora at Calvin's Pharmacy and Fifties Soda Fountain after Lynley's day in court. Though there had been tears over the divorce, there had also been plenty of healing laughter among dear, longtime friends.

And now Lynley was faced with this. And handling it poorly.

"She's ruining her life, cutting herself off from the world." Kirstie accepted the tissue Megan handed her.

"She's here taking care of her mother. That's how she sees it."

Kirstie held Megan's gaze. "Is that how you see it?"

"I deeply admire what she thinks she's doing, I just don't agree with the way she's going about it. She can't be on guard 24/7, and that puts you at risk."

"That's what concerns me," Kirstie said. "What if something happens to me the next time my brain unexpectedly plunges me into Capps Creek? Not that I'm afraid for myself, because I'm as sure of my afterlife as you are of that stethoscope you live with, but I'm mother enough not to want my daughter to endure that pain."

"Something happened to you this time."

"I wasn't terribly maimed. Somehow, I almost wish I had been at least slightly more injured. I should've never given her power of attorney."

"You can always check yourself into a care center. I know of a good one in Springfield."

"I tried that. Didn't Lynley tell you? I went to Scrieb's Health Care, had most of the arrangements made, started to sign the papers and had a brain glitch, right there. Can't remember anything but fear and loss. They called the emergency number I'd just given them, and wouldn't you know, Lynley came, showed them her DPOA papers and brought me back home. I was, of course, back in my right mind by the time she arrived to pick me up, but would anyone listen to me? She warned them that she would see to it that they would not receive funds to care for me."

Megan's annoyance with Lynley dug a deeper groove as she prepared a syringe and tubes for drawing blood. Why was Lynley risking her own mother's safety to defy a doctor's diagnosis? Where was *her* brain these days? And what made her think she was the only one capable of caring for her mother?

"Don't blame her," Kirstie warned, reading Megan's expression with obvious ease.

"We need to get you checked into a safe place before something bad does happen to you and her whole life is corroded by guilt," Megan said. "We could at least hire someone to work nights and keep watch, or we could rig up some kind of alarm system on your door."

"It wouldn't have helped last night. I wasn't inside the house. I apparently just walked off the front porch without my shoes or anything. And no one can watch me every minute."

Megan handed her friend another tissue. "I'll drive you to Scrieb's myself."

"I'm on their reject list."

"Take back power of attorney."

"I'd rather not do anything that drastic."

"You can stand up to your own daughter, Kirstie." Megan said it, but she wasn't sure she meant it. Lynley was the darling of Kirstie's life, her only child, the source of her joy. Just as Alec was to Nora. Kirstie and Nora had a lot in common. Perhaps that was why they'd been so close for so many years despite their conflicting personalities. Kirstie would do anything to keep Lynley happy and safe.

Wasn't that what most mothers did? The defining term was *most*. Megan sighed and withdrew her thoughts from that old and aching sore spot.

"What's to stop Lynley from threatening nonpayment to the next place you try to check into?" Megan asked.

Kirstie suddenly focused her attention on Megan. "I have some ideas. Meanwhile, tell me when that gorgeous man out in the waiting room showed up."

For a few seconds, the subject change caught Megan off guard, though it shouldn't have. Kirstie often did that when she wanted to take control of a conversation.

"You're deflecting," Megan said. "This office visit is about you, not me, and I'm not finished talking about you."

"He drove all the way from Corpus Christi to see you, didn't he? What did I tell you last week?"

"Give it up, Kirstie. It isn't going to work."

Kirstie's grin, though strained by the effects of the night before, was genuine. "I warned you that your heart was in danger, but I can see the warning came far too late."

Megan positioned the syringe. "I'll have Carmen prepare a medical release form for you to sign before you leave today so I can get your records."

"Not Carmen."

"Why not?"

"I want you under the radar. No one needs to know you're taking the case."

"You're talking crazy."

"True to form, according to some."

"That isn't what people are thinking, Kirstie. Your friends and neighbors are simply worried about you, so why keep all this under the radar?"

"I have my reasons," Kirstie said. "Let's get back to the more interesting subject. Don't tell Nora I said so, but I think her son has some formidable competition. Why is it you always seem to be dating your boss?"

Megan tightened the tourniquet around Kirstie's arm, thumped for a vein, held the needle up and wiggled her eyebrows in a gesture of lighthearted teasing that she hoped reached her eyes.

"Don't even try to threaten me with pain, Megan Bradley." Kirstie made as if to reach for the syringe. "I can draw my own blood if you're going to tease like that."

Megan fixed the needle tip in a healthy vein and started the draw. "I'm not dating the boss now and I never dated Gerard."

"But you spent a lot of time with Gerard, right?"

"Naturally. He runs the mission."

"But you ran the clinic, so why did you spend so much time with him?"

"The clinic is inside the mission. He was in the clinic a lot. He cared about the people who came in."

"And about the doctor who treated them." Kirstie's voice turned gentle. "He cares a great deal about you."

"We live in different worlds."

Kirstie sighed. "Have it your way. Carmen saw you with Alec at the drugstore lunch bar Friday, and Nora just happened to mention it several dozen times when I had coffee with her yesterday. She's always had her sights on you for her son. You think she'll welcome Gerard to town?"

"Alec's married."

"That was a spur-of-the-moment decision he's regretted ever since. Did he tell you they knew each other three weeks before they got married? Too sudden and too short. Nora barely met Zoe before the separation."

"But there's been no formal divorce yet."

Megan felt bad for Alec, but he would never be more than her boss. Not now.

"The girl's been gone for a year. It was a nonmarriage as far as Nora is concerned."

"Anyway, it wasn't a date, Kirstie. Alec just wanted to catch up. We hadn't seen each other for a while." Megan kept her focus on what she was doing and didn't look up.

"Nora also mentioned in as many casual ways as she could that you had lunch with him at Corinne's Café Monday. I'm telling you, she's got her hopes up."

"He and I are friends, okay? We do have history, and I guess he just needed to talk about things. I was always a good listener."

"So no romance this time around? No kisses exchanged?"

Megan sighed. "He started to kiss me and I turned my head, so he caught me on the nose. Real romantic."

Kirstie laughed out loud.

"I think we both proved to ourselves that there was no lasting romance there." Megan hadn't meant to make any comparisons, but it had happened despite her intentions. Even after returning to Jolly Mill, after knowing Gerard Vance and seeing the ocean depth of his heart, becoming reacquainted with Alec was, for her, like dipping toes into the kiddie pool. Though she knew he had matured since their breakup, she also knew his depths weren't for her to plumb.

"To hear Nora tell it, he broke your heart and didn't realize until afterward that you were the one for him," Kirstie said. "Besides, you two were kids when you were dating."

"We dated for two years. We had other classmates who were dating then and are still together now. It wasn't meant to be."

"Things change when you've lived life for a while."

Megan took a long, deep breath. "That's right. An adult learns to take things slowly and grow a friendship."

"You mean the way you and Gerard did." Kirstie fiddled with the pillow under her head. "Nora will press the issue, of course. You know she will. She'd like her son to see a lot more of you. I hope you realize that's why you're staying for free at their cottage. Nora hears wedding bells."

"Nora hears the patter of grandchildren feet."

"She dotes on Alec too much. That concerns me because a doting mother does not a good mother-in-law make."

"Never underestimate Nora Thompson."

"Not that you can repeat this," Kirstie said, "but after

Alec's marriage went south, Nora pretty much decided he needed help with his next choice."

"Parents should never play matchmaker for their kids." Megan shuddered at the thought of her own parents doing that to her. She would rather remain single the rest of her days than let Griselda Bradley choose a pair of shoes for her, much less a man. Not that Griselda would ever do that kind of shopping with her daughter. They could never spend quality time together as mature adults without allowing sewage of a dirty past to come between them.

"Now that we've caught up on the vital gossip and I know you won't explode with it," Megan said, "why don't we refocus on your health right now? You'll be helping Lynley if you help me."

"I want a complete toxicology screen on this blood you're drawing," Kirstie said.

"Got it. But you know that won't cover every possibility."

"I know. We can test for more later if we don't come up with anything this time around. And I don't want Carmen to know. Under the radar, remember?"

"But that's impossible, Kirstie. For goodness' sake, Carmen's in the other room."

"So is Lynley. Probably checking out your new suitor."

"He's not my—"

"Don't you dare try to lie to me, Megan Bradley."

"Carmen is bound to know if I run the tests you want me to run. And she's one of your best friends. What's she going to think—"

"She won't think anything I don't want her to think."

"Ha!"

"Don't forget I know my way around this clinic. I can file the forms I need for my medical records from Springfield. And I don't want you telling Lynley anything either. This is strictly between you and me and one other person."

The drop in Kirstie's typically bright voice put Megan on edge. "And who would that other person be?"

Kirstie fixed her with a firm, Kirstie-knows-best glare. "You won't like it, but you're my doctor, and unless you fire me from your service—"

"How can I fire you from my service if no one even knows I'm doing this?"

"I need you to keep this quiet."

"Kirstie…"

"Other than the three of us, I'm demanding strict confidentiality."

"The three of us would be you, me and…?"

"Gerard. I want you and Gerard Vance to work together to figure this thing out."

Gerard was on his second cup of coffee, deep into an explanation about his plans for the rehab center and manufacturing plant, when Carmen took a sudden breath, nearly choked on her coffee and waved her hand in the air.

"Oh my goodness, Lynley, I know just the place he needs, don't you?"

Lynley placed her mug of tea on the table beside her and leaned forward, elbows on her knees. "You're talking about Uncle Lawson's property, right?"

"For the rehab center," Carmen said. "Wouldn't it be perfect?"

"It would need some refurbishing." Lynley narrowed her eyes, obviously considering Carmen's suggestion. She turned to Gerard. "You would have passed the place on your way into town from Megan's cottage this morning. It's a huge rock and wood structure on the side of the hill to your right, across Capps Creek."

Gerard felt his eyebrows rise. Lynley had thawed.

"It's called The Barnes Lodge and Resort," Carmen explained. "Kirstie's uncle used to operate it, and he was so successful that he entertained dignitaries from across the country. It's gorgeous, with beautifully appointed suites, a ballroom, banquet hall, restaurant, a conference area, grand staircase, the works."

"I see there's an airport not ten minutes from here."

"You've been doing your homework then." Carmen sat back. "You'll need to check that out. So," she said, crossing her legs and getting comfortable, "what happened between you and Megan anyway?"

"Carmen." Lynley rolled her eyes and shook her head at Gerard. As if she hadn't recently asked the same question. "She gets like this sometimes. You know how small towns are, don't you?"

"Of course he does," Carmen said. Her green eyes sparkled with undeniable mischief. Friendly mischief. "Megan said he grew up in one. Gerard, Megan's told us so much about you, it's like finally meeting a movie star. So are you and Megan going to make things work between you?"

It was Gerard's moment to nearly choke on his coffee. "I don't think there's anything Megan and I can't work through."

"I still don't see Megan moving back to Texas," Lynley said.

"You say Kirstie's uncle owns this resort?" Gerard placed his cup on the table and gave up trying to finish it. He had, indeed, forgotten what it was like to live in a small town, but he was quickly recalling a few things.

"That's right. Lawson Barnes," Carmen said. "He's wealthy and he likes to spread the wealth around. If he knew what you were doing, he might even donate at least part of the property. Don't you think so, Lynley?"

The younger woman hesitated. "You'd have to talk to him while he's still alert enough to understand."

"Lawson has lung cancer," Carmen told Gerard.

"He's been in long remissions twice over the years, and he's fought a good fight." Lynley's voice wobbled. She swallowed and took a breath. "But he's been advised by his oncologist to get his affairs in order."

"I'm afraid I'd feel like a vulture if I approached him about it now," Gerard said.

"I think he'd be interested in doing business with you," Lynley said. "He's still carrying on as usual, and he really is trying to get his affairs in order. He's a wonderful person with a huge heart. A rehab center sounds like something Uncle Lawson would want for the resort."

"You wouldn't be the vulture, believe me," Carmen said, with a meaningful look at Lynley.

Lynley grew still for a moment. She closed her eyes, and when she opened them again they were silvered with tears.

"Sorry," Carmen said softly.

"Does he have any kids?" Gerard asked.

Lynley shook her head and dabbed at her eyes with her fingers. "Just a niece and a nephew, Mom and her brother, Arthur."

Warning bells went off in Gerard's head. Kirstie was set to inherit apparently a lot of money and she suspected poisoning, and it was just now being mentioned? Why hadn't Kirstie said something earlier? "If your great uncle were to donate the property, or part of it, that would mess with your mother's inheritance."

"Mom always believed that too much money could ruin a person."

"And you?"

"I can make my own way. I'm not like my father. I

don't pretend to be friends with the rich uncle and then wait around for him to die so I can inherit." Lynley's voice took on a bitter heaviness.

"Your father's named in the will?"

Lynley nodded. "Mom doesn't want to tell Uncle Lawson that Dad's left her. He and Dad were hunting buddies for a lot of years, and Mom doesn't want to break Uncle Lawson's heart right here at the end."

Carmen shook her head. "Kirstie's too good-hearted. She's more interested in protecting everyone but herself."

Gerard felt himself clenching and unclenching his fists. How true Carmen's words were. He may be a newcomer to this mess, but from his first meeting on the phone with Kirstie he'd realized Barry Marshal never deserved his wife.

"I'd like to take a look at this place," he told Lynley. "Where is Mr. Barnes? How would I contact him?"

Lynley got up. "I'll go write down his information for you, but Mom has keys to the place. I know he won't mind at all if you take a look at it." She entered the glassed-in office.

"Count yourself an honored man," Carmen said softly. "After what she's been through, I wouldn't expect her to trust another man to tell him that much about her struggles."

"You do know I can still hear you, don't you?" Lynley asked, sliding the reception window open.

"Sure do, sweetheart."

Before the two women could exchange more friendly fire, two car doors closed in the parking lot.

Gerard glanced out the plate-glass window to see a dark-haired, exotic-eyed woman in a dress of emerald silk. She carried a large leather bag over her shoulder. She turned from a champagne-colored Cadillac Seville and strode toward the doors. The heels she wore were at least four inches high. Gerard imagined a model on a runway would envy the graceful movements.

A younger man with those same dark eyes slipped ahead of her to get the door. Mother and son. This would be Nora and Alec Thompson. They both looked friendlier in person than online.

Gerard rose to his feet as the woman stepped inside.

Carmen rose with him. "Nora, tell me you brought them. You promised."

Nora nodded and pointed to her bag as her attention settled on Gerard. "Can anyone tell us how Kirstie is?"

"Megan's patching up her feet," Carmen said. "She's back in her right mind. Nora and Alec Thompson, meet Gerard Vance. He's—"

"I know who he is." Nora stepped forward and held her hand out. "He's definitely a Texan."

Gerard took the hand. She had a solid handshake, a level gaze, a husky voice. She was another of Kirstie's trusted friends, and she was an impressive woman who seemed capable of handling multiple enterprises successfully.

Alec followed in his mother's wake. So this was Megan's new boss in person. His grip was no less solid, and his smile seemed genuine. He made no attempt to display machismo by squeezing too hard. "We've heard a lot about you since Megan went to work in Corpus Christi." He had a gentle baritone voice. "We've all admired what you're doing down there. A man's got to have a calling for that."

Gerard nodded. "It's good to finally meet some of the friends Megan always spoke of with so much fondness."

"Megan tells me she still owes money for her loan since she left the mission early," Nora said. "We're hoping her salary here will help pay that off."

"She doesn't owe me anything," Gerard said. Why did she have to make him the bad guy in this? "She never has. That was a government loan with the agreement that she would work with the underprivileged and underserved for two years after her residency. The government could require she pay back every bit of her loan if she doesn't complete all her time. I'm concerned she may also incur penalties for leaving early."

Gerard could almost hear the internal gasps of the people in the room. There was so much Megan hadn't told anyone.

"How much could that amount to?" Alec asked.

"Let's just say she could be several years paying it off by herself, even with the efforts her friends here are making on her account."

"So then why would she leave with so little time left to complete the requirements?" Nora asked.

"Working health care at a homeless mission is a burnout job," Gerard said. "She's worked long hours to help people who end up back out on the street. So many people she treats are drug addicts and alcoholics with no interest or ability to improve their situation. They'll die early and she can't do anything about it. Many homeless people have mental illnesses and can't help themselves."

"Didn't you tell her what she was getting into before she accepted the loan?" Alec asked.

"I told her."

Nora placed a hand on her son's arm. "You know our Megan. She wouldn't have listened. She thinks she can change the world if she only has a chance."

"Until she'd had a taste of the frustration," Gerard said, "she had stars in her eyes about helping those most in need of help."

"The stars are gone." Nora shook her head. "It seems

she's lost something vital. I just don't want to see her in debt for years."

"I have a plan," Gerard said. "If it works, she'll be okay." He glanced in the direction he'd seen Megan disappear. Was it his imagination, or was she taking an extra long time with Kirstie back in that exam room?

size a lot something what I just don't want to see her in that for years.

".....have a plan," Gerard said. "If it works, she'll be okay." He glanced in the direction she'd seen Vickie doing.... such as what his impression of was she taking as little long time with Kirstie back in that exam room.

SIX

Megan pulled a set of medium-size scrubs from the cabinet by the door and stepped to the exam bed to help Kirstie change out of her mud-stiffened nightgown. The exam room smelled like fish. They'd managed to get a great deal of the mud from her hair and skin while arguing about Gerard's presence in this case. Kirstie wasn't typically a manipulative woman, but today she was pulling strings like a puppeteer.

"You've told me yourself that he still behaves like a cop." Kirstie slid her feet into the scrub bottoms and allowed Megan to pull them up and tie them. "Who better to help you if there's danger involved?"

"How about Sheriff Moritz?"

"He doesn't have a clue about all this."

"You might be surprised what folks around here know of Barry."

Kirstie looked up at Megan. Their gazes locked. Megan would never tell Kirstie all she knew about him.

"You suspect him too, then," Kirstie said.

"Right now I hate him and I want to find him guilty."

"Oh, honey, you don't want to be filled with hatred. It'll only hurt you."

"We're focusing on your health right now, not mine."

Megan resisted the urge to roll her eyes. Kirstie had a lot in common with the Vance family—forgiveness, love, kindness, all the things that supposedly kept a person emotionally healthy. "Besides, I can't forgive Barry right now, and I don't think Lynley can either. Can you?"

"I'm trying." Kirstie placed a hand on Megan's and squeezed. "That's one of the things keeping you from Gerard, isn't it? The depth of his faith? While you're still mysteriously angry with God after all these years?"

"Let's talk about what's going on with you. Barry didn't leave when you had breast cancer. So why leave this time?"

Kirstie sighed. "He told me it was because he couldn't face watching me change. He didn't feel he should have to remain with someone who was no longer the woman he married."

"And yet he let his own daughter face it alone. What man would do that to his wife and child?" If Barry was here right now, Megan would be sorely tempted to scratch out his eyes.

"A weak man."

"And stupid," Megan said. "To leave you now? Not to sound crass, but you stand to inherit millions soon. I can't see Barry ever forgetting that."

Kirstie's hand slid from Megan's. She closed her eyes. "Maybe he was just so desperate to get away from me that he didn't care. Or maybe he's afraid the cost of caring for me for years will eat up the money."

Megan slid a pair of the clinic's paper shoe covers over Kirstie's injured feet. "He cares about the money, believe me."

"And yet he cared nothing about hurting the woman he should love most in the world." Kirstie shook her head.

"There's the bite. He should have loved me, but how long has it been since he has?"

"My question isn't why he doesn't love you, but whether he's ever been able to love. Kirstie, I've never seen him show true affection for anyone, not even his own daughter." Megan knew she wasn't telling Kirstie anything she didn't already know. "I'm not sure why he spent so much time hunting with Lawson, but I can guess. Perhaps Lawson should have protection."

Kirstie closed her eyes. She took a deep breath and let it out. "I told myself when I first suspected Barry of being a player that I'd made my own choices and I would have to live with them. Marrying the man was one thing, but having a child with him? Unconscionable. And his friendship with Lawson? It was because of me. You can't imagine how much guilt I've lived with all these years." She looked up at Megan. "You think he'd be vile enough to try to hasten Uncle Lawson's death?"

"Until he's dead, Lawson can always change his will." Megan moved around behind Kirstie to give her some privacy as she slid the nightgown off and pulled on the scrub top.

"Despite his many, many faults, I can't imagine Barry ever trying to kill his hunting buddy," Kirstie said.

"That's because you always want to believe the best of people. It's why Lynley's such a loyal, good person. You raised her to be just like you."

"I know our marriage has lacked in a lot of areas, and my fight with cancer weakened what connection we did have, but I have to say I was shocked when he left me."

"Why?"

Kirstie grimaced. "You and I both know Barry worships money even more than he worships women. But he knew Lawson was dying and that we would inherit a bundle. Why would he leave me before Lawson dies?"

Megan shook her head. "It doesn't make sense." She'd expected him to leave Kirstie years ago, and he probably would have if not for Lawson's money. Barry neither understood nor appreciated his wife's Christian belief system, and throughout their marriage he had taunted her for her faith.

Though Megan had long ago barred her heart from conversations with God, she believed there was something to the biblical concept of believers not marrying nonbelievers. That, in itself, was a good reason to avoid Gerard. Their most basic belief systems would clash.

Kirstie gave a soft sigh. "Maybe seeing me like I am just repulsed him so much he couldn't stand—"

"There's nothing repulsive about you."

"Maybe to a man, reconstructive surgery just isn't the same."

"A real man would love his wife even more, would be grateful he hadn't lost her."

Kirstie paused. "And you know this how?"

"Gerard told me."

"So you do see Gerard as a real man."

"Well, he's—"

"A man's man. Tough and gallant and able to punch through rocks for the woman he loves."

Megan grinned and gave Kirstie's shoulders a gentle squeeze. "Don't get carried away."

"Um, honey, you used those very words once a few months ago. And I do remember them. No trouble with recall there. So you must understand why I want Gerard to get involved in this. He not only thinks like a cop, but he'll also know how to protect you while you work on finding out what's really happening to me—which is definitely not Alzheimer's."

"I did tell you I have a license to carry, didn't I? And that I know how to shoot? Gerard taught me."

"But you're not a cop, and I hate to say this, honey, but you're no fighter. I doubt you'd be much good at hand-to-hand combat. Plus there's the issue of Gerard's investigative abilities—something you also talked about when you were more willing to admit your attraction to him."

"Now I wish I'd kept my mouth shut."

"Impossible when a girl's in love." Kirstie turned around on the exam bed, swung her feet over the side and took Megan by the arm. "It'll be safer for all of our friends and loved ones here if Gerard's around to keep an eye on things."

"Where's he going to stay?"

"He can stay in my guest bedroom. Now, I'm going to wash my face a little better and then snatch your former employer for a ride home. I'll tell Gerard all about it. He already knows the basics. I trust him to take the blood samples to a lab in Springfield—and me to the doctor's office to get my records." She studied Megan's expression. "You look worried. Afraid I'll steal your man from you before you change your mind about him again?"

"Of course not."

"Well, trust me that you're going to change your mind. You've got a winner there."

"Obviously you think so."

Kirstie gave her a wink. "Help me up."

"Wait until I finish packing these samples."

"So you're up for my plan?"

"For you, Kirstie." And she hoped Kirstie would some-day appreciate how difficult this would be.

* * *

Gerard listened as Carmen recounted to Nora and Alec his plans for the rehab center and manufacturing plant. Nora tapped a manicured finger against her cheek as she studied him with those dark, astute eyes. The mother was obviously the brains behind the Thompson businesses. Or at least the power.

Alec's expression had darkened the more Carmen talked. He hadn't spoken enough to reveal much about his character, except to show a touch of anxiety about Gerard's relationship with Megan. Which meant Gerard could have some kind of competition. He tried not to think too much about that for now. Later, when he knew these people better, he'd be able to read them more clearly.

He couldn't, however, ignore the curious glances he continued to receive from Alec as Carmen spoke.

"Do you have concerns about the plans for the rehab center, Mr. Thompson?" Gerard asked when Carmen paused to take a breath.

"Call me Alec," the man said. "I wouldn't say I'm concerned as much as curious. I've never heard of a rehab center for the homeless. What would it offer?"

"Room and board initially. Placement would happen after we're settled."

"Would there be any training involved?" Nora asked.

"All kinds. For some, it could involve helping our people get their GEDs. Others might need on-the-job training, which some are already receiving in our Texas facility. Still others may need to complete college and get diplomas."

Alec whistled softly. "You do all that?"

"We've already started things in motion."

"Your family is all involved?" Nora asked.

"My brother, Hans, runs the plant in Texas now, and I

run the mission. Our sister, Tess, and her future husband, Sean, will take over the mission in Corpus Christi when I establish a place for our newest project."

"But how will you know which people to bring to the rehab center?" Nora asked.

"We have families with children living in cars or on the street because of lost jobs and inability to pay mortgages, and that's not just in Corpus Christi—that's all over the country. Those people will be our first targets. My dream is to make this nationwide."

"Children on the streets?" Nora exclaimed.

"Women, children, teenagers who once lived what they believed to be the good life," Gerard said. "My initial goal is to bring those people who are employable but who have no place to live and give them a home here where it's safe and peaceful. I want to get their children enrolled in school and support them while the adults help take over the running of the facility."

"In other words, you're putting them to work right away," Alec said.

"That's the most vital thing we can do for them after feeding them and putting a roof over their heads. They need that self-respect. Our motto at the mission is taken from the Bible: If they don't work, they don't eat."

"Isn't that a little harsh? What about those who can't work?" Alec asked.

"Why would an adult be unable to work?"

Alec shrugged. "Injuries, mental illness."

"We're not slave drivers. We don't force people with back injuries to lift heavy weights, but they can help with food service, bookkeeping, whatever they're capable of doing, and that helps them retain their self-respect. Our goal isn't to continue giving handouts to the same people—it's to get those people back on their feet and help them become contributing members of society again."

"Bravo," Nora said. "I think my son is concerned you're going to bring a bunch of freeloaders to town and ruin the community."

Alec scowled. "My mother is putting words in my mouth."

"Good words, though," Gerard said. "I invite your questions. In fact, after I do some investigating, I may decide to request a town hall meeting and open the floor for questions."

"I don't think you want to do that here," Alec said.

"Why not?"

"Because you'd be changing the whole character of Jolly Mill."

Gerard had to admit to himself that the man seemed to truly care for this town. "I understand that you don't want to lose what you have here, but what if the changes were positive? Those who have lost jobs in the recent past here in Jolly Mill would have more job options. We could work together to make this town stronger."

"How can you guarantee you won't bring troublemakers?" Alec leaned forward, elbows on his knees. "I'll admit my mother has a point. What if these people lost their homes because they weren't willing to work hard enough to save them in the first place? What if the same thing happens to them here? We can't afford a homeless population in a tiny town like ours." Gone was any veneer of friendly curiosity.

Megan had said that Alec and Nora were good people, and she should know. But there were often good people on opposing sides of an argument, and Gerard had to check his own tendency to distrust Alec. After all, hadn't the man lured Megan from Corpus Christi with the promise of a job? What did he really want from her?

"We will do background checks on every family under consideration," Gerard said. "My brother can tell if he's getting a good employee or not."

"I think if anyone can get it done," Nora said as she pulled the elegantly tooled leather bag from her shoulder, "you and your family would be the ones to do it, Gerard, according to Megan, and I trust her opinion. I think it's admirable and it will help a lot of people." She ignored a glance of irritation from her son. "This town needs more people with your kind of compassion and ambition." She cast Carmen a companionable grin. "With the energy of youth to carry him, right, Carmen?"

Gerard studied the resistance in Alec's expression. Was he seriously doubting the plan, or was he doubting the man who would be implementing it?

"I'm not coming here to take jobs from established members of the community," Gerard said, "but to bring hope. With my family's plans to extend our manufacturing business to this area, we'd hope it would not only help with unemployment, but will keep those from the rehab center employed so there are no homeless."

Alec held Gerard's gaze. Definite animosity there. Jealousy, perhaps?

Despite his interest in the subject, Gerard couldn't help casting glances toward the treatment rooms, hoping that Megan would walk out with Kirstie at any moment, proclaiming Kirstie to be in fine shape, perhaps to announce a sudden discovery that the medications Kirstie had been taking after her cancer turned out to be the culprit for her memory loss.

One could dream. He knew Kirstie had been checking into that.

Alec was still glaring with suspicion when Gerard looked back. Not surprising. Nobody wanted a stranger to come into their town and start talking about bringing a boatload of changes—and there would be changes with so many new people moving here. If it happened here. Gerard shouldn't blame Alec for his wariness.

But how close was his friendship with Megan? She and Alec had known each other since kindergarten. Obviously, they'd known each other well.

Alec hadn't requested any kind of recommendation from her former employer about her skills as a physician. What kind of man would hire a physician to care for people, no matter how well he knew her as a person, without some kind of input from a former colleague or employer?

This situation would need to be handled with finesse in a town so small and close. Gerard had to be able to get along with everyone from the beginning. And he needed to make sure they all understood that he and Megan had a solid relationship and that there was definitely no room for anyone else in Megan's life. Hers was already full to bursting. He definitely needed to make that obvious.

Of course, first he had to make sure it was true.

As Megan finished packing the blood samples for shipment, Kirstie sat on the bed and combed her fingers through the hair they'd tried to clean with wet towels. "Believe it or not, I'm not playing matchmaker here, though I can't help believing he'll turn out to be the man for you when it all comes out in the wash."

"I'm not going there."

"He's real all the way to the core. You've said so yourself on numerous occasions, and I've checked him out online and talked to him. He also loves you."

"Kirstie—"

"I know that isn't something you'll talk about right now, so we'll let it slide for the moment."

"You keep trying to divert my attention, so what aren't you telling me?"

Kirstie reached forward and delivered a mild thump on the side of Megan's skull. "Use this thing, sweetie. You and I both agree that it's possible I'm being drugged or poisoned, and I am not delusional. Anyone who would do that to me would do as much or more to you. I want you protected. I want Lynley protected."

"You honestly think Barry would hurt his own daughter?"

"It may not be Barry, honey."

"Don't go soft on me. You've admitted you know what he is."

"It isn't that simple. I think it's possible someone believes that if I have Alzheimer's, with my short-term memory whacking out on me, my long-term memory may kick in at unusual times. Someone may fear that I'll remember the wrong thing at the wrong time."

Megan frowned at Kirstie.

"It's possible I witnessed something without realizing what it was," Kirstie said.

"Here? In Jolly Mill? I don't think so."

"You don't know."

"Anything in particular on your mind?"

Kirstie hesitated. "If I tell you, I'm afraid you might decide I'm truly nuts."

"If I'm going to play spy doctor, it would help if I know what you think is happening."

Kirstie straightened her legs and looked at her shoe covers without the shoes. "I've always taken pride in my feet. Maybe that's because I was once voted to have the prettiest feet in our class in high school. Of course, Nora had the prettiest eyes, but I've always taken extra good care of my feet, making sure my shoes fit just right, getting my pedicures every month—"

"Now you're really scaring me. What does this have to do with—"

"*Something* is scaring *me*," Kirstie whispered, glancing toward the door. "Memories or impressions of some kind seem to be reaching out to me from the past—incidents that I never connected together before, but for some reason I'm connecting them now."

"Do they involve your feet? You're losing me, Kirstie."

"I don't typically go running barefoot through the woods. I don't think I would do that, even in the middle of an altered state of consciousness, unless I was terrified. I may not be able to remember what happened to me last night, but I'm recalling bits and pieces of other things from years ago."

Megan took a slow, deep breath and waited, heart rate climbing.

Kirstie leaned closer to Megan. "When I'm on the verge of slipping out of reality, I can tell it by a blast of fear. I discovered that just this morning, when I came to myself in the darkness, poised above the creek with my feet in pain."

"You remembered something you haven't before?"

"I could tell dawn was near, and I tried to make my way down toward the creek to find out where I was, but the fear came over me again, and I realized, just before I fell and hit water, that it was a familiar fear."

"Familiar in what way?"

"There's an impression of something black and evil looming over our town."

"But you're saying it's a memory from the past?"

"I caught a glimpse of it this morning, Megan. When I hit the water, I snapped from the blackout, and just for a moment I was connected to both worlds. And there seemed to be a connection to all the other blackouts I've had."

"What did you glimpse?"

"Do you remember Mara Trillis?"

"Yes. She went to school with Lynley and me. She drowned in the mill pond when she tried to swim drunk."

"I've seen her," Kirstie said.

"In your blackout?"

Kirstie nodded, maintaining Megan's gaze. "In the corner of my eye when I was sinking into one of my dark spells. Beautiful young girl, big eyes and…other attributes. You and Lynley saw her that night, before she drowned, and you tried to talk her into coming home with you so you could sober her up."

"She refused."

"You and Lynley always blamed yourselves for that, and I reminded you that without knocking her in the head and dragging her home, you could have done nothing."

"What does Mara have to do with your blackouts?" Megan asked.

"What if my mind is forcing me to recall some things in the past to help me figure out what's happening now? Face it, honey, sometimes my subconscious is all I have left but I believe it's working. Long-term memories are still working. If not, then I'm totally insane and without hope."

"Maybe it's just a bad dream?"

"Not a dream, but a bad memory I can't get rid of. Sometimes when I close my eyes I get this feeling that I'm not alone," Kirstie said. "Someone's watching me. If there's something to be afraid of, I don't want Lynley anywhere near me. I want her safe. I think that's why I run without any consideration for what I'm doing to my poor feet. I think I'm afraid. Terrified of something that this other part of me—the crazy part—isn't ready to share with my conscious."

"You're saying you may have seen something you shouldn't have, and someone knows it? That you're being poisoned…drugged…to confuse you or make you lose credibility?"

Kirstie closed her eyes and nodded. "It's possible," she whispered. "Or it could be possible that while I was in an altered state of consciousness I remembered the wrong thing and may have told the wrong person, and now I'm in danger."

"Oh, Kirstie. But here in Jolly Mill?"

The watery eyes opened again. Kirstie nodded.

"You're saying you think Mara could have been murdered?"

"I'm just saying we're not immune here any more than any other place on Earth."

"But you have nothing more concrete?"

Kirstie shook her head. "All I can remember is that part of me is convinced it's something real. I keep getting this vague impression of a circle, but that could just be my mind telling me I'm going around in circles," she said dryly.

"Mara was found near the arched section at the bottom of the mill where the mill wheel turns. It has a somewhat circular entryway, and the mill wheel, of course, is circular. Could that be what you're remembering?"

Kirstie spread her hands. "I wish I knew. I want to know the results of those tests as soon as you get them, but I don't want anyone else to know you took them."

"Okay. I'll do it."

Some of the color returned to Kirstie's face. "Thank you. I know how much it'll cost you. Maybe my mind is playing tricks on me and I'm in denial about these blackouts," Kirstie said, "but I can't take the chance, not if there really is something wicked happening in Jolly Mill. If no one knows you've taken my case, then you'll be safer. As for Gerard, he can't be the bad guy because he isn't even from here. I've suspected for years that my husband was befriending Lawson because of the money."

"You're no dummy."

"Lynley told me what Mara said the night you two saw her."

Megan's movements froze. "What did she tell you?"

Kirstie looked at her. "Don't you remember?"

Megan nodded.

"So what did Mara say?"

Megan's throat was suddenly dry when she swallowed. "I'd rather you tell me."

"She asked Lynley where Barry was because he'd dumped her like an orange peel."

"Oh, no," Megan whispered. "Why would she tell you that?"

"She simply told me the truth. It was a burden too heavy for her to bear alone."

"You remember the words so clearly," Megan said.

"It isn't something a woman forgets."

"Mara was drunk. I told Lynley not to listen to her."

"Mara was dead the next morning, and you know how that affected Lynley. Of course, Barry had come in late the night before."

Megan packed the tubes of Kirstie's blood and filled out the order forms for testing, then slid the whole packet into the wide side pocket of the scrub pants Kirstie wore.

Would the blood have stories to tell? Had Barry suddenly gotten greedy?

Megan looked at Kirstie, and the expression of betrayal in her eyes said she could be thinking the same thing.

"If we divorced, he wouldn't get any of the money. If I died, he'd get it all," Kirstie whispered.

SEVEN

Feeling self-conscious about the package in her pocket, Kirstie followed closely behind Megan into the waiting room to a chattering committee of five. Gerard—all six feet three inches of him—sat between Lynley and Carmen, and the three of them faced Nora and Alec.

Everyone stopped talking and looked up at Kirstie.

It didn't look as if Alec was overjoyed by Gerard's presence, and Kirstie couldn't blame him. Alec had grown into a handsome and intelligent young man, but he did still have a marriage license hanging over his head without the benefit of a wife, and no married man would ever have the opportunity to come between Gerard and Megan—not if Gerard had anything to say about it.

Megan stiffened beside her, and Kirstie gave her a sideways glance. Ah. Yes. Megan confronted with the only two men she'd ever loved. Of course, she was only a kid when she was dating Alec, but puppy love could be a powerful emotion. She'd grieved for a full year over their breakup after she and Lynley went away to college.

Carmen appeared to have taken Gerard under her maternal wing. A little too closely. Nora beamed at Gerard as if he'd just agreed to run for office on the Nora Thompson ticket.

Kirstie Marshal, shame on you!

What had they all been discussing before the grand entrance?

Gerard stood up. "Kirstie? Everything okay?"

"Good as new." Kirstie's voice held not a hint of a tremble, and she prayed everyone would be too distracted by the hideous mudpack in her hair to take note of the square package partially hidden by the hem of her scrub top.

She glanced again at Megan and suppressed a grin. The poor girl couldn't get her mind around the room. The whole room. It not only contained two men she probably hadn't wanted to ever see together, but it also held her close friends, who she certainly did not want to deceive. Kirstie would have to do some more convincing, it was obvious. Or ask Gerard to do it for her.

"I trust introductions have been made?" Kirstie said, taking over the conversation. "If not, Gerard—"

"We've met and had a lively discussion." Nora's husky voice filled the room with her presence as she stepped to Kirstie's side and reached for her hair. To her credit, she didn't react to the fishy smell. "Kirs, I simply must introduce you to my hair stylist. He's the best, and could he ever do something with this mop."

Kirstie chuckled and swatted her friend's hand away. "Even my cats could improve this mop, and I'm not driving farther than Monett for my haircuts. Jenni's an artist with my hair. Now, let's see who's going to have the honor of taking me home so I can become human again."

Nora leaned forward to lay an arm around Kirstie. "My car's outside at your service."

For a moment, Kirstie hesitated. How comforting it would be to just let go and allow Nora to take care of everything the way she usually did. But even Nora needed to be protected from this.

"Goodness, no." Kirstie grinned at her oldest friend. "I'm sure you have gourmet treats to deliver, and I need a big, strong man who can run me down if I get out of line, and Nora, even you can't run in those heels."

"Nonsense." Nora eyed the bandages and booties on Kirstie's feet. "I didn't just rip my feet into hamburger like you apparently did. If need be I'll put a leash on you."

Gerard smiled and stepped to the women with a wink at Megan. "I'll do the honors, ladies, if you don't mind."

Kirstie studied the man. If she didn't know better, she'd think he owned the town. He had the confidence and grace of a man much older. Self-assurance was something Megan had struggled with as a teenager and probably still did from time to time. With Gerard, it seemed he was in his element wherever he went, not just in the state of Texas.

When Kirstie glanced at her daughter and saw that even Lynley didn't protest his offer, she had no further doubts about Megan's man.

"I need to get to work," Lynley said. "Thanks, Mr. Vance."

Kirstie hobbled from beneath Nora's half-embrace, trying not to wince with the pain. "Thanks, Gerard, I accept. I want to hear how that rescue mission of yours is doing without you today. Our Megan can be so close-mouthed about herself, but I know she must be truly missed."

"You can't imagine how much." Without missing a beat, Gerard held his arm for Kirstie to grasp, nodded to the others, glanced at Megan. "Come and fill me in, Doc. Tell me about any damage I need to watch for."

Kirstie turned to glance at Megan, who followed the two of them out the door, her pretty brown eyes pensive. She didn't appear surprised by the tender care with which

Gerard treated Kirstie. He'd likely helped Megan in the mission clinic plenty of times.

"Don't worry, Lynley," he called over his shoulder as the door swung shut behind them. "I'll take good care of her."

"She found no evidence of a concussion," Kirstie informed Gerard. "And as I told Megan, I didn't inhale anything from the creek. All I need is a nice hot shower to scrub the dirt and smell away."

"That'll be interesting if you plan to keep those bandages clean," Megan said.

"You think I can't rebandage my own feet?"

"Take your time." Gerard walked with her to the passenger side of his car and helped her in. "Obviously you were wounded. I saw evidence of the blood."

"That wasn't from the fall—it was from running barefoot over rocky ground for who knows how long."

"Why would you do that?" he asked.

"Same old blackouts, only this time I wasn't wearing shoes, and the crazy part of my brain wasn't thinking, 'Hey, let's put shoes on to protect our feet before running through the woods like Bigfoot.'" Kirstie paused and turned to look up at Megan. "I'll explain it all to him, honey. You just keep Lynley calm today, okay?"

"Will do."

Gerard made sure Kirstie was comfortable, then closed the door and turned to Megan. To Kirstie's guilty joy, his passenger- and driver's-side windows were open. Obviously, the man didn't worry much about having his car burglarized. But of course, she'd explained to him how peaceful Jolly Mill was, with hardly any crime. A mad poisoner, perhaps, but other than that, not much.

"Meet with me after you get off work?" Gerard's voice,

though softened, reached through the open windows. "We have a lot to talk about."

"I wondered what you were up to out in the waiting room while I was back there battling blood and gore." Megan's voice held a hint of a drawl. Humor.

Kirstie grinned. A good sign. Megan had nothing to be cheerful about unless she was secretly glad she was being forced to spend time with Gerard.

"May have a place for the rehab center," Gerard said. "I've told you often enough that when God has a plan, it's going to happen."

Kirstie felt another load moving from her shoulders. The man was an active believer. His influence would be doubly good on Megan. Kirstie would see to it that Jolly Mill had something to offer by way of a rehab center and land for a manufacturing plant.

"I'll be out of the clinic by five," Megan said, "probably earlier because our schedule isn't full. I'll be hungry."

There was a slight hesitation, then, "You're not teasing me, are you?" Gerard asked. "Because earlier this morning—in fact, less than an hour ago—I was pretty sure you wanted me to go back to Texas."

"We have more to talk about than you think. Kirstie will fill you in. We're going to have to see this through."

"Will do." Another pause. "Your boss stop by the clinic often during the day?"

Kirstie pulled her seat belt down and buckled it as she grinned. Eavesdropping. A wonderful occupation.

"Didn't you come to the clinic all the time at the mission?" Megan asked. "What's the difference?"

"There are more employees here. You have plenty of help without a nonmedical person."

"If I owned a business, I'd want to keep watch over it and make sure things went smoothly." The humor was still present in Megan's voice. Perhaps she picked up on the jealousy too.

Oh, yes, there was a romance going on here to beat all romances, and Gerard Vance had a strength of character Kirstie had not seen in quite some time. Certainly not in Barry. Gerard didn't strike her as the kind of man who would leave the woman he was committed to for any reason. He would stick with her to the death. He wouldn't find another woman to leave her for either, like Lynley's so-called man had done to her.

Megan and Gerard may have some hurdles to overcome right now—though Kirstie had not yet been successful in wheedling those out of Megan. Maybe she would have better luck with Gerard. She doubted it, but she could try.

Megan pressed her lips together, but she knew Gerard could read the expression in her eyes. She shouldn't be pleased, or even amused, that Gerard was so obviously jealous of Alec, especially because she didn't want him believing he had the right to feel that way or that there was anything to be jealous of. Still, something about his interest spread her insides with warmth.

"He may be my biggest challenge as I attempt the rehab center," Gerard said. "He's not on board with it, though his mother seems to be."

"Then you've no worries," Megan said. "Nora's the one who has the heart of the citizens. What she says usually goes."

"You sure about that? You've been back what, three weeks? After being gone for fourteen years? Things change."

"And you've been in my town what, an hour? And you think you know my lifelong friends better than I do?"

A light of challenge glowed from his blue eyes. "Plain

old common sense tells me that folks from this town will honor a man who is a hero in their eyes. He fought for them in the war, he had a tragic loss and he was born and raised here. That has all the makings of a town leader."

"Well, Texan, I think you've got some fans here yourself," Megan told him with a grin. "Carmen seemed taken with you, and of course Kirstie." She leaned close to his shoulder. "You're about to find out just how taken she is with you. I hope you're packing heat."

"Weapon? Sure."

She smiled. "Not that you'll need it at doctors' offices, but she'll be impressed. Even Lynley didn't bite your head off, and she hates men right now."

"Well then, I guess if it's up to the women, you may soon be looking at the new director of the Jolly Mill Homeless Rehab Center, and the new plant manager for Vance Industries, employing those rehabbed folks."

Megan's mouth went slack. "You mean you've already decided? I thought this was just a hunting expedition."

He held out his hands. "I said you *may* be looking at him. You may not. We'll see."

She narrowed her eyes at him. There was a tiny expression of discomfort around his mouth. Not everyone in the room had fallen at his feet in adoration. This was not the time to tease him, as she would have teased him at the mission. She would never gloat at a man's misfortune, but he was always so self-assured that sometimes she felt just a twinge of satisfaction when she was reminded of his humanity. He was not indomitable.

"I don't suppose you could feel him out a little…" Gerard spread his hands. He looked almost humble.

"Sorry, I can only do one spy job at a time."

Gerard's brows went up. "You're spying now?"

"Talk to Kirstie, and keep in mind that I'm a doctor. I never signed up for undercover spy work."

"Believe me when I say I don't want you doing this under covers of any kind."

Megan laughed up at him, and as if he couldn't stop himself, Gerard gazed down at her, eyes lit with his own brand of humor and a generous helping of tenderness. He touched her cheek with his hand. "I think you can get through to him."

"About what?"

"About how much a manufacturing plant and a resort refurbished into a homeless rehab center would help the town with tax income."

"His mother can tell him that. And I think that would sell a lot of people at a town hall meeting."

"Think we can get one called?"

"We? Nora has most of the committee members in her back pocket, and as you've said, she's obviously sold on you. No problem there."

"Okay, then anyone else you speak with in town. I'm sure you have a lot of friends."

"I do." At last, Megan felt a tug of regret for her recent lack of support. This was a step she knew Gerard had wanted to take for so long and for all the right reasons. How could she not admire a man who stood strong for his convictions and fought hard to see them through? Even if she didn't want him here, in this town, constantly reminding her of her own fears and her own loss.

He raised a thick blond brow at her. "We will, of course, need a doctor nearby for the center."

"Everyone needs a doctor."

"And you know if our people traveled up here from the mission, they would be immensely relieved to find you here, someone they know they can trust, who cares for them. They'll be apprehensive about their futures."

"They have you," Megan said. "They'll feel safe."

"Do you feel safe with me?"

"I never feel safe."

"Then you know why another familiar face will help."

"No. Familiar faces aren't helping me." Megan glanced toward the car and knew without a doubt that Kirstie had just heard what she'd said. Blast Kirstie's good hearing. Megan cast a glance back toward the clinic. Patients would start pulling into the lot any time. She didn't want to have this conversation.

"You know how much we miss you, Megan," Gerard said. "I'd love to have your help."

"Why don't we deal with today's problems before we dive into something months or years down the road? I know I'll eventually have to complete my contract to pay back the government loan by serving in an under-served community. Could we keep it on the back burner for now?"

"He doesn't have a clue you're here on medical leave, does he?"

"Who?"

"Your boss."

"He needs a doctor, and he has one."

"I've found it's best to be honest as possible with your employers." The gentleness in Gerard's voice once more warmed her.

"Nora and Alec already know that part of my reason for being here is for Kirstie."

He took her hand and squeezed it, surprising her. Actually, her response surprised her—making her feel all tingly and squooshy and everything she did not want to feel.

Physical attraction was such a difficult enemy to battle when one needed to remain detached.

Despite that need, however, Gerard was still so obviously excited about the possibilities of the future that she had an impulse to hug him the way Tess would have, to give him a sisterly hug. But that would have to wait, especially if he was going to be working closely with her for the next few days…weeks… Who knew how long it would take to discover what was happening with Kirstie? Who even knew how bad she would get before they could find the real culprit?

"I'd better go inside and get to work."

He looked down at their clasped hands and released her. "So I'll see you tonight?"

"I'm sure you will."

"I'll give you a call later." He glanced toward the downtown area. "Any place around here with good food?"

"I have a feeling you'll have no lack of invitations from the ladies who'll want to get to know our latest import a little better."

"I mean with you. Alone."

"Our diners in town close before dinnertime."

"Your place then? Soon as you get off? I'll bring the food."

"Kirstie can direct you to the right restaurants in Springfield."

"I'm going to Springfield?"

Megan sighed. "I told you, talk to Kirstie."

"It's going to be okay, Dr. Bradley. It'll work out."

"You trying to convince yourself of that?"

"Just you. I have faith it's going to work out." He took a step toward her, bent down and kissed her cheek. "You're not alone in this, Megan. I'm not leaving you alone."

She held her breath as she watched him walk to his car,

and when she finally inhaled, the air smelled sweeter. She stood watching as he got into his car, backed out and drove a brightly waving Kirstie out of the parking lot and toward her home past the bridge on the hillside opposite the grain mill.

Waiting for her heart to retrieve its normal rhythm, Megan sauntered back to the front door of the clinic to find, of course, that everyone there was incapable of minding their own business. She stopped just inside the door. It felt as if all the oxygen had escaped the room.

Alec was in the same spot where he'd been standing when Megan followed Gerard and Kirstie outside. "Megan?" Alec's deep timbre drew her gaze. "Gerard says he's still your boss."

"He *was* my boss. Big difference."

"But he said that if you don't go back to work for him, you could be in trouble with your loan agent. Why would you leave a job like that when you only had three months left to work? You don't want to get into trouble with the government."

"Would you relax? A girl has every right to take time off after working for 21 months straight with hardly a day off and very few evenings."

"It must have been a meat grinder," Carmen said from the reception window.

More than they could know. "I do have some leeway," Megan said. "I didn't want Lynley and Kirstie to have to struggle with the diagnosis alone after Barry turned into a feral tomcat and decided he couldn't handle his wife's illness." She glanced at Lynley, who was pretending to work a few feet from the reception window. "No offense meant, Lynley."

Her friend joined Carmen in the window. "I think I'm

the one who initiated that term in the first place. So you're taking Mom's case after all?"

"I told everyone several times that I'm not a neurologist. I'm a friend, and I will be here as a friend. So I'm here, okay? I fixed her feet. Nora, are those cookies I smell? I'm starved, and I haven't had a minute to eat."

Nora held up her designer shoulder bag and smiled, her perfect white teeth even, lips touched with just the right shade of deep pink to blend with the glow of her tanned face. Nora Thompson was a strong woman who Megan always believed could move mountains by force of will.

Though Alec had inherited a great deal of her strength, he was his own person, not just a blend of his strong mother and his nonpresent, hotheaded father. Alec held his special set of values that he'd been forced to develop early because of his father's abandonment. Megan hadn't been home long enough to judge whether or not his values had seasoned over the years.

Though she'd dated him steadily for two years, his values and hers had never blended well when it came to physical expressions of affection.

Alec fell into step at Megan's right shoulder as she followed Nora toward the break room. "Are you going to go back and complete your contract?"

"I don't plan to go back, no. I've told you this." Megan's stomach growled nearly as loudly as her voice. She was glad that, during the two lunches she and Alec had shared together, they'd spent most of their time catching up on the goings-on in Jolly Mill and talking to the other diners— the majority with whom Megan had spent her childhood and teen years.

When asked about his wife, Alec had made no reference to any divorce proceedings, and she'd let that subject drop. In apparent gratitude, he didn't ask personal questions about her life either.

Megan joined Nora in the break room to avoid more questions from Alec. Nora knew her way around the break room—Thompson money had built it. She washed her hands and pulled a serving platter from the cabinet to the left of the sink and commenced arranging her cookies.

At fifty-three, Nora had the physique of an athlete twenty years her junior. She swam, practiced martial arts and gardened, which gave her the tan. Of Mediterranean descent, she had the ability to tan without burning or wrinkling, and there had been a long rivalry among Nora, Carmen and Kirstie about who would go completely gray first. Carmen cheated, of course, as did Kirstie, but Nora didn't have a single streak of white in her thick black hair, not even at the roots.

"You should eat some protein first." Nora's voice was warm and buttery-sweet. "But since there are eggs in the cookies, and I could hear your stomach from down the hallway, you should fill it with something before you get dizzy and pass out."

Alec stood at the entrance and braced himself against the door frame. "If this morning's appointments are anything to judge by, you're in for a long day."

"Busy morning, light afternoon," Nora said. "Megan, your...former boss is good-looking." She spared a glance for her son, whose gaze slid over Megan's face.

Alec had eyes as dark as his mother's, but his strong chin and light brown hair were those of his father. He had the face, physique and charisma that could make a girl forget herself...and her inhibitions...and her own dreams, if she let her guard down. Megan had not, even as an impressionable girl. She had her mother to thank for that, at least, though not for the right reasons.

Megan bit into the crunchy dream of one of Nora's most recent entrepreneurial accomplishments. Her saucer-size gourmet cookies had become a stock item in coffee shops throughout the four-state area. This black walnut–butterscotch was Megan's favorite.

Nora turned and leaned against the counter edge, and for a moment two sets of exotic eyes beheld Megan—Alec studying her with as much curious intensity as his mother was.

"What are we going to do about this situation?" Nora asked softly, glancing past her son toward the hallway. There was no sound of approaching footsteps.

Megan didn't pretend to misunderstand. "I think Lynley will change tactics before long. This morning's incident got her attention."

"It should have," Nora said. "She's like a kid trying to prove she's all grown up."

"She is grown up."

"She isn't behaving like it right now. She's your best friend, hon. Can't you convince her she's endangering her mother?"

"Gerard's with Kirstie now. He'll keep a close watch over her."

"Oh, yes, that man is definitely an enigma, isn't he?" Nora studied Megan for a few seconds before glancing at her son. "Quite the charmer. No wonder you were so taken with him, and I can't believe you left with only three months left on your contract."

Megan suppressed a sigh. "Gerard told you that, did he?" She was going to kick him in the—

"You know we'd take care of Kirstie. You didn't have to come running immediately."

"I know."

Nora crossed her arms. "So what brought you here at such a run?"

"Didn't Gerard tell you that too?"

Alec entered the room at last and reached for one of the cookies. "I don't think we've heard the whole truth yet."

"You try working in a mission clinic and see if you can last two years."

"Try fighting in a war while your wife's playing single back home," Alec snapped.

"Well, why don't we have a big ol' knock-down-drag-out right here close to medical aid?" Nora said. "Mind your manners, kids. Kirstie does need help until we can get this thing worked out. I've promised her that if she would just move in with me for a few weeks I'd hire a housekeeper/bodyguard for daytime and chain her to me at night, but would she do it?" Nora shook her head. "Stubborn woman. Have you convinced her to see a neurologist, Megan?"

"Not yet."

"Why on Earth won't she go? I tell you, sometimes I want to smack her silly she's so stinking bullheaded."

Megan took another huge bite of the cookie and stepped to the window that overlooked the mill and the pond. She loved this view. She also loved having a full mouth so she couldn't be expected to answer any more questions for a moment.

"Kirstie could afford to hire someone to watch over her at night so Lynley can at least get some sleep," Nora said. "Alec wants to keep her and Lynley here at the clinic as long as they can stay. All the patients are comfortable with them, everyone knows them, and that means a lot, having a hometown entity caring for your medical needs. Besides, Kirstie's my best friend, and I want to get to the bottom of this so she can get on with her life."

"Do you think those two stubborn women would agree to accept some help?" Alec asked.

Megan swallowed and shrugged as she turned back to them. "They've both been knocked sideways by Barry's abandonment. I think she's more concerned about Lynley's feelings than her own safety."

"Then talk to Lynley," Nora said.

"Gerard's going to be around for a few days, and he's already been offered the private guest suite upstairs at Kirstie's."

"Drat that woman," Nora said with a grin. "I knew she'd snatch him right out from under my nose. When did she talk to him?"

"I believe they've been in contact by phone and email."

"How did they meet?" Alec asked.

Megan squeezed her tongue between her teeth. What was this, an interrogation room? It was supposed to be a break room. She shot Alec a crooked scowl.

"Right," he said. "I'll ask Kirstie."

"Thank you. I believe Gerard will watch over her while he's in town, so maybe you could make him feel a little more welcome."

"Excellent idea." Nora picked up the platter, left some cookies behind and carried the rest from the room.

EIGHT

By the time Gerard pulled into Kirstie's driveway she had given him a succinct rundown of this morning's episode, her talk with Megan and her desire that only Gerard was to know anything about her suspicions.

He glanced at the interesting cat decorations in her three front windows. One of them moved and jumped to the ground. Feline voyeurs.

"I know something's going on with that girl," Kirstie continued in that mellow, soothing voice that, despite her circumstances, tended to make one think all would be well. "Listen to me, calling her a girl. She's a grown woman."

"I know, but she's like a daughter to you."

"And to you?" Kirstie asked, looking up at him. "What is she to you?"

He felt a smile grow across his face. "A dream come true."

"That's what I wanted to hear." Kirstie unbuckled her seat belt. "She'd have already told me if not for these wicked blackouts."

Gerard jerked when a white blur of cat jumped onto the hood of his car, then he looked at Kirstie in confusion. "Told you what?"

"Why she really left you. I'll warn you right now, I'm an eavesdropper. I didn't even have to try to overhear your conversation in the parking lot because you both have voices that carry well. She had good reason to leave that mission, and she hasn't breathed a word to anyone about the reason. She seems to think she's protecting me from the truth. She has a tendency to place her own needs last."

"She seems to be following your example."

"Care to tell me what's up with her?"

"I'm sure when Megan is ready to tell you, she will. Until then I'll respect her privacy."

Kirstie's gaze rested on two more cats as they jumped down from their perches on the windowsills and ambled toward the car. "Spoken like true husband material."

Gerard battled opposing emotions of apprehension and elation. He trusted Kirstie's insight. And that was all the reason in the world to feel joyful and apprehensive. "Poison, huh?"

She reached into the right front pocket of her blue-green scrubs and pulled out a package. "My blood. You won't mind taking me to Springfield today to have it tested? Especially if I promise to speak to my uncle about the resort property?"

"Forget the property. If you think there's a chance we can find out what's really going on with you, that comes before anything else right now."

Kirstie opened her car door. "In that case, would you keep Prissy, Poppy and Data company while I clean up?"

"Data?"

"The white one with black splotches." She gestured to the inquisitive cat with yellow eyes who was making dust tracks on the hood of the car.

"You like *Star Trek: The Next Generation*." Gerard nodded toward the cat.

"You're a fan of the show?"

"I even attended a convention." Gerard rushed from his seat and around the car to help Kirstie to the house.

She took his arm and allowed him to help her. "You know, I've been opening my own doors for a lot of years, and I don't intend to stop now, but I do appreciate an attentive man. I have to admit my feet are killing me." They waded through cats to the front porch.

"I'm not really a cat person," Kirstie said as she stepped aside to keep the prettiest calico female from tripping her. "I rescued Data from the top of a truck tire at a truck stop out on the interstate. Couldn't find a home for him despite the cuteness factor. Prissy and Poppy haunted my windows and doorstep for a month before I gave up and took them in. No one would take them."

Gerard grinned. "How hard did you try?"

Kirstie chuckled. "Not hard enough obviously. They're my buddies. It's strange that sometimes the cats all gather around me, as if they're afraid I may be getting ready for another blackout."

"I've heard of animals doing that."

"They'll all jump onto my recliner and perch on my lap, my chair arms, touching me and purring, despite the fact that they're typically so jealous of each other they won't stay on the same chair all together."

"You've charmed them."

"No. As Dean Koontz once wrote in one of his Christopher Snow novels, cats know things."

No doubt they did. Gerard gestured at the broad covered porch. "This is where you were last night before you blacked out?"

"It was my last clear memory. Data was, as usual, on my lap. Poppy was chasing ants on the concrete and Prissy was curled up in the other chair."

Gerard studied the two beautiful calicos as they danced around Kirstie's feet. "And Lynley?"

"She was inside studying at the desk. I think she had fallen asleep before I wandered off into the night. I'm so worried about her."

"But there's hope that you can be helped. That's a good thing."

"True. But what if it's too late? Or what if I'm wrong?"

He looked down at her and frowned. "That doesn't sound like the Kirstie I've come to know."

"Wait until you're a mother."

He grinned and opened his mouth for a flippant reply and then closed it again. She was right, he couldn't identify with her motherhood. He knew she agonized about her daughter as he agonized about his family, those people who depended on him...and Megan.

Kirstie didn't know what Megan had endured, but she understood it was something bad. The four people he'd spoken with in that waiting room also understood it now. He'd made sure they did. He only hoped they would be insightful enough to understand that Megan needed her space right now. Anyone who knew Megan well would realize something catastrophic must have happened to force her from the mission and the people she loved.

And he hoped she would be insightful enough to realize he could help her through this and that she really did love those people.

But first, they had to get to the bottom of Kirstie's blackouts. As he stared down the hillside at the mill pond, it suddenly seemed urgent that they get to Springfield and place Kirstie's blood into the right hands as soon as possible.

Alec reached down and chose one of the remaining cookies on the platter his mother had placed on the break room table, then glanced at Megan. "Mom's good at what she does, which is controlling people." He held the cookie up to the light, as if studying it for ingredients.

Megan winced at the sharpness in his tone. He and Nora both had hard-charging temperaments, and they had struck sparks off one another for as long as Megan had known him.

He sighed and shook his head. "Sorry. I need to take the edge off my temper, don't I?"

He could still read her. "I didn't say that."

"She plays a good mommy role," he said.

"Oldest sibling syndrome, Alec. Being an only, you wouldn't understand."

"She tries to carry the world on her shoulders," he said. "No one is Atlas. People who try will break beneath the strain."

"Some people are just wired to protect and help others."

Alec held her gaze in silence for a moment. "Your expression still gives you away, Megan. You're talking about your latest crush? Your former boss is the mommy type?"

"Crush? Really? I'm not a teenager anymore."

"Okay, then, the former boss who raced from southern Texas to see you? Mommy type?"

"Gerard's more patriarchal than matriarchal." She thought about all the talks she'd had with Gerard. Standing in the hallways…discussing patients in the clinic, welcoming his help when there wasn't enough staff to keep up with the onrush of patients…in the kitchen, helping prepare a community meal when not enough helpers showed up—which, granted, wasn't a typical incident. The local churches had able and willing volunteers who helped support the mission with their time and finances.

"Strong man." Was there a hint of mockery in Alec's voice?

Megan felt her lips curve up. "You wouldn't tease about that if you'd seen him break up fights and toss troublemakers back out onto the street."

"Good with people, huh?"

"He is."

"And you admire him."

"I do. He's kind of a mix between a preacher and a bouncer, if you can imagine."

"A praying man, then?" The mockery in Alec's eyes disappeared.

"He prays. He reads the Bible. He talks about God's love to the people who must have more trouble than anyone believing in the existence of a god of any kind in their worlds."

"Do they listen?"

"He has a way of getting to them." He'd almost gotten to her. Probably would have if a killer hadn't come between her and God.

And why was she talking to Alec about Gerard? Alec had obviously given him a bad time. Megan broke off another piece of cookie. Nora was always experimenting with new ingredients. The chocolate chip oat nut was Megan's second favorite. This was her favorite.

"So maybe he's one of those people who doesn't take on the weight of the world, they hand it over to their Source of strength."

Megan paused, unable to mask her surprise at the words she'd have never expected to come from Alec's mouth. "You sound as if you've had some experience with that."

"A guy's belief system is tested when he thinks he might die at any moment, when death waits behind every rock and around the corner of every shack or building in a country that is foreign in all possible ways."

"How did you do it?"

He shrugged. "I'm my mother's son in some ways. I gritted my teeth and bore it, did what I was told. But I also prayed."

Megan blinked. Sure he did.

"Come on, Megan, the same church van took us both to Sunday school. We do know how to pray."

She walked to the window and stared out at Nora's garden just below the windowsill. The woman loved beauty, and she loved to share it with others. Maybe she was an overindulgent mother, and her overcompensation had taught Alec to expect everyone to meet his demands. Odd to hear him talking about spiritual things. But he seemed to have changed a great deal from the macho jock she once thought she loved.

Years ago, the night of graduation, for the final time, she refused to give in to his pressure and he broke up with her. If only she'd realized at the time that he'd done her a favor. They'd been great friends, but they weren't suited for more than that.

"You don't believe I could ever be a praying man." Alec had stepped up behind Megan in his silent way.

"I guess your prayers were answered. You're home safely."

"What do you call safe?"

Megan glanced over her shoulder at him, glad he wasn't invading her space. Glad he'd learned that valuable lesson.

"I wasn't wounded physically." His voice had gone quiet. "But then, I lost half my heart."

"Nora told me your wife left you soon after you were deployed. I'm sorry."

His attention switched to the garden, and in the morning light Megan could see for the first time how the past few years had caught him in their unforgiving jaws. He hadn't aged much in the face, but there was bleakness in his eyes that she'd never seen.

"I thought she loved me enough to wait for me to come home. Word reached me overseas that she was partying in LA less than a month after I left."

"It's an awful thing to happen to a person protecting our country. Are you expecting her to come back?"

He shook his head, still staring into the garden. "You never met her. She wasn't as…" He glanced at Megan, then away. "She wasn't as considerate as you are, but then, who is? She's always liked the city. I guess she had second thoughts after the ceremony when she realized she'd be stuck here in Jolly Mill forever."

"She moved away with another man?" Megan had heard Lynley talking about it.

He nodded.

"Let me guess…he had money."

Alec winced visibly, and Megan felt a stab of anger at the woman. She recalled Tess telling her about Gerard's fiancé breaking their engagement when she discovered she wouldn't be living a life of lavish spending on his family's money, that he was using his wealth for more important things. But he'd been a member of the Corpus Christi police force when he was engaged. That should have given the woman some clue that he wasn't just engaged to her, he was engaged in life, in helping others.

Alec's glance swept over Megan as he turned from the window. "I'd have thought you would feel avenged."

"What? No. I'm thirty-two, Alec, not seven."

His eyes closed, and his square jaw clenched as sorrow etched him. "I didn't mean it to sound like that." He picked up a cookie and handed it to her. "What I meant was that it's probably what I deserved after the way I treated you."

"No."

"How can I make the past up to you?"

She didn't take the cookie. "You gave me a job. That's enough. Let the past stay where it belongs."

"I was worse than a jerk to you."

"You were a teenager with raging hormones. You're a different person now. Give yourself the break your wife never seemed to give you."

"I thought she would file for divorce, but since the marriage contract doesn't mean anything to her, obviously she doesn't see a good reason to dissolve it."

"Is she waiting around for you to inherit?"

Alec gave her a genuine smile. "Probably. Thing is, because the Thompson empire isn't mine yet and because Mom's young and healthy, and I don't earn a large salary, that won't work. When we had to lay off people at the casket factory I took a cut in pay."

Good. If the woman married Alec for his money, she must have discovered Nora's firm hold on the businesses after the ceremony. "You still love her?"

"Maybe I do. If so, that makes two lovesick men in this town right now. Vance must want you back pretty badly to come all the way here."

"That's what he told you?" Megan reconsidered the cookie. She picked it up and took a bite.

"Oh, no. He wouldn't show his hand like that."

"He told me you weren't in favor of the homeless rehab plan."

"I'm not. I don't want Jolly Mill to be a different town when more of our soldiers return home."

"I'm sorry you see it that way. This plan of Gerard's could help a lot of people."

"Maybe. But his first thought is for you. He's a man willing to do whatever it takes to follow the woman he loves."

Megan snatched another cookie for later and turned to walk from the break room. "You might want to try that yourself," she said over her shoulder.

"Why? Because it worked on you?" he called after her.

A grin blossomed. She didn't reply aloud. It was time to put Gerard out of her mind, difficult as that seemed right now. She wanted to recheck the exam room where she'd treated Kirstie and make sure everything was cleared away and no evidence was left of the blood tests she'd taken.

But as she entered the empty room she heard Alec's footsteps behind her. "Did he tell you about all the things he's planning to do to Jolly Mill?"

Okay, now he was invading time Megan couldn't afford to lose. "I don't think he was sure it would be Jolly Mill, but of course I know what he's planning. He's spoken of it often. It's been in the works for some time."

There were no signs of the recent activity that had taken place in the room. The tubes of blood had been concealed on Kirstie's person. The order form was filled out and ready for the lab, and Kirstie could call ahead to the doctor's office in Springfield for her medical records. Nothing here gave away their quietly constructed strategy.

Megan spotted an alcohol swab on the corner of the counter, covered with Kirstie's blood. "I think you may want to do a little more research before you make any decisions."

"I don't like what I've heard so far."

"Because?"

"I want Jolly Mill to remain Jolly Mill."

"Of course you do." Her words were sharp, and she took a couple of seconds to curb her tongue. "No one wants change," she said more gently. "But you traveled to the other side of the world to risk your life for people who weren't even your countrymen. Now Gerard's offering our town a chance to make a difference in countless lives, to return them to productivity. Trust me—he does things right." She paused as she thought of Joni, but even Gerard couldn't control everything. It occurred to Megan that it seemed a whole lot easier to forgive Gerard than herself.

"I don't want to let our own people down either," Alec said.

"Just think about it, and while you're doing that, where's a good place to eat dinner out these days?"

He seemed relieved by the subject change. "You still like Cajun food?"

"Only if it will melt my tongue."

"You could try The Bayou in Monett, if you think Gerard could handle it."

"He's from southern Texas. They all like it hot down there." She gave the exam room a final look and then turned to leave.

Alec placed a hand on her arm. "Wait. Megan." His voice was soft enough to not reach Nora, Lynley or Carmen, who had their heads together in the front office. She caught the scent of his bergamot soap—she knew he used it because Nora gave him a year's supply of the stuff every Christmas. He either liked the scent himself, or didn't care enough about it to change. Megan used to love that scent, but she'd forgotten it over the years. It did nothing for her now.

"I know we never talk about the past," he said. "Small talk seems more our style this time around."

"This time around?" She looked up at him.

"What I'm trying to say is I know there was something between you and Vance, but you came home, right? Obviously, that story hasn't ended happily, no matter how he seems to feel about you."

Megan sighed. "That story hasn't ended yet."

"Your choice or his?"

She narrowed her eyes. "You pretty much told me you're still in love with your wife. Why do you care about my relationship with another man?"

He took a deep breath, put his arms behind his neck, stretched and exhaled. "Did you stop to think that maybe the reason one man would follow his beloved halfway across the country and another man won't isn't because of the quality of the men, but of the women? You'd have never abandoned your vows."

"No. I wouldn't." And she'd have never married a man for his money either. "Neither of us has called off the relationship." She hesitated, realizing the words she was about to say were true and that they frightened her. "There's still a story between Gerard and me."

NINE

Kirstie slept on the drive home from Springfield, her seat back nearly horizontal, Gerard's sweatshirt serving as a pillow beneath her neck. Gerard envied her. Though he'd never in his life fallen asleep at the wheel, he felt his eyelids growing heavier the closer they drew to Kirstie's house. How had Megan made it through residency with so little sleep? How did any doctor live through residency?

He pulled into Kirstie's drive and studied the large house of pale gray brick with insets of dark brown stone. Shaded by mature oaks, maples and cedars, the house was built into the cool cliff overlooking Capps Creek. At Kirstie's urging, Gerard had already carried his suitcase to the guest suite upstairs before they left for Springfield. He would have free reign of the upstairs and full use of the upper deck that overlooked the creek. From there one could see most of the town, and he could also use the outside stairway so he could come and go without intruding on Kirstie and Lynley.

When he switched off the engine, Kirstie awakened as if on silent alert. She adjusted the seat into an upright position. "I love your car. It rides like a dream. Literally."

"Thank you. Why don't you continue your nap while I make some calls and plan some meetings? I appreciate the opportunity to meet Lawson today. That was a nice surprise." He could tell Kirstie was grieving heavily for her dying uncle, and now, after an opportunity to get to know the man, he could see why.

"I thought you two should meet, Gerard, and I think you gave him hope." She unbuckled her seat belt and opened the door. Twice Gerard had attempted to get the door for her when they were in Springfield, and twice she had gently told him he did not have to coddle her as if she were an elderly woman.

Data—her black-and-white cat with eyes the color of gold foil—and the two calicos, Poppy and Prissy, came trotting out from beneath the trees to greet their mistress, tails held high. Data once more leapt onto the hood of the car as easily as a helium balloon. Ears perked forward, he sniffed toward Gerard and then sniffed at the car. Kirstie obviously had a way with animals, just as she had with people.

She yawned and plucked Data from the hood. "Sorry. You may have to put up with this nosey boy while you're here. He'll also perch at your upstairs windows and talk to you. He always likes to be higher than anyone else, and these kitties are all three voyeurs." The cat nuzzled her face and cuddled against her shoulder, and Gerard could hear him purr.

"I live on a ranch with horses, dogs, cats and ranch hands," he said. "A few cat tracks will keep me from being homesick."

"Oh? And I figured you came up here because when you're with Megan, you are home."

He grinned. "I feel kind of pulled apart right now, but things always feel that way when they're about to change."

"What did Uncle Lawson say about your plans for the rehab center?"

"He asked a lot of questions about the mission in Corpus Christi."

"To get a feel for your ability to manage such a feat. I'm sure he was impressed."

"He isn't an easy person to read, but when I explained what I was trying to do with the rehab center—resettle the families and working people who'd lost their homes in the economic crisis—he seemed engaged."

"You want to separate those who are innocent and vulnerable from the more hard-core street inhabitants."

"You must have eavesdropped again." On the drive to Springfield, Gerard's conversation with Kirstie had been about her discussion with Megan in the exam room this morning. He'd mentioned very little about his plans for the rehab center because Kirstie's was the more pressing need.

"No, I stayed out in the garden with Aunt Lydia, but Megan's told me about it in detail."

"She has?"

Kirstie gazed up at him with gentle eyes. "You really don't know, do you? That girl is crazy about you even if she hasn't been able to admit it lately."

The woman's words were a soothing balm to him. "We've talked about it a lot. In fact, Megan has shown a great deal of wisdom with her ideas on how to go about making the change, sending a few job hopefuls at a time to Vance Manufacturing to shadow the workers there— which we've already begun to do—bringing house staff to learn about operating the living quarters and kitchen services for the trainees as we build the new plant near the rehab center."

"These were all Megan's ideas?"

"She wouldn't admit it, of course, but I'm not sure I'd have come up with as workable a plan without her input."

"In other words, you two have a symbiotic relationship."

He thought about the murder. Would that tragedy continue to hover in the way of the new hope he believed they could find here? Would it destroy the symbiosis?

"So this company your family started so many years ago, it's like a creator of giant Lego?" Kirstie asked.

Gerard chuckled. "Our detractors accused my father of that when he first began the business years ago. It took quite a bit of explaining to make the public understand that our home-building materials weren't just giant building blocks but the possible wave of a future designed by an architect who understands the financial challenges a safe and sturdy home can be on a growing family. With so much bad weather blowing away mobile homes in our area of the country, folks want something safer that doesn't cost more than they can pay. We applaud their fiscal conservatism, and so our recycled materials are built strong to endure bad weather and are designed in a way that when the family needs more room, the home they already own can be expanded easily with the simple plans that would connect to the initial house."

"Your brother, Hans, runs the plant in Texas?"

"He's grooming someone to fill his shoes so he can take a more active role in the rehab center and manage the setup of the new plant."

"So he may be coming here? I'm warning you, Gerard, if he's anything like you he may need to watch out for the cougars."

"Cougars?"

"You know, older women who like younger men. You saw how shamelessly Carmen behaved this morning."

"She was charming. Don't talk about your best friends that way."

"I heard Hans was widowed a few years ago," Kirstie said.

"He's never quite recovered."

"One never does recover completely from losing a spouse—no matter the loss."

"You miss your husband?"

Kirstie shook her head. "I've never recovered from losing him, but I lost him many years ago. Want some lemonade?"

"No, thanks. You should rest."

"I think you should warn your brother that there are some beautiful women in Jolly Mill who look forward to meeting him. Throw him to the cougars. If he's as tough as you, I believe he can handle them." She led the way up the steps to her front door. "Any sales in the offing?"

"Sales?"

"Sorry, I get like this sometimes. Sleep deprivation. My mind flitters from place to place like a moth surrounded by candles. Be glad you'll never be a menopausal woman. I was merely wondering if you and Uncle Lawson had worked out any kind of agreement, and I distracted you with the subject of Megan, and of course you seem to always be distracted by Megan. Any sales in the works?"

"Not yet. Lawson wasn't what I expected."

"I know. He doesn't act sick. He's tough as a boot, but he's been given two months at most." Kirstie opened her front door.

"I like him," Gerard said. "I like to take my time and study things, but he made some good suggestions, and he seems engaged. He did warn me I may have some conflict from the townsfolk."

"Of course, but I think you're the kind of man who thrives on deftly handling conflict."

Gerard chuckled as Kirstie disentangled Data's claws from her blouse and dropped him to the carpet in the entryway.

Kirstie fingered her wavy blond hair from her eyes. Some women aged well; some didn't. She was the kind of person whose age didn't show on her face but whose maturity showed in the wisdom in her eyes, in her laughter, her ability to see past the present trials of her life.

"You'll need to talk to the town council about zoning changes," she said. "I imagine when folks find out what you're up to, you'll have some strong supporters and some powerful naysayers, but Uncle Lawson will definitely be an ally, I can tell you that. He wouldn't have asked you so many questions if your plans didn't interest him. He's not the type to waste precious time on being a people pleaser."

"I think he's excited about the thought that his resort might be used to help so many."

She led the way to the kitchen. "Having all those empty rooms sitting there for so many years has weighed on him, I know. I asked him several times why he didn't sell it, but he always loved that place and didn't want it to go to just anyone. It would take serendipity to make it sing again. That's why I wanted him to meet you."

"You think this is serendipity?" Gerard asked.

"I think it could be. I want it to be. I want Uncle Lawson to feel that his final weeks on this earth counted for something before he goes on to Heaven."

Gerard understood. He had seen providence at work a few times in his life, and he knew how to recognize the signs of God's handiwork, but he didn't want his hopes to get ahead of God because he'd done that before and been busted. Still, it wouldn't hurt to start the process of talking up his plans to the townsfolk and see about rezoning.

"You have a few hours to work on that before Megan's off," Kirstie said. "Meanwhile, I'm going to take a nap so I'll stop scaring you with my stream-of-consciousness chatter. You won't have to babysit me because the only times I've had my blackouts I've been tired from lack of sleep. Obviously, I don't black out when I'm sleeping. Don't wait for Lynley to come home. You're not here to be my guardian." She reached into a cabinet and pulled out a keychain with several keys on it. "These are for you."

He took them from her. "What are they?"

"Entrance to the resort. The keys are labeled. Uncle Lawson would want you to look it over carefully. Maybe you and Megan can check it out later this evening." She gave him a little wave and turned toward the hallway to the master suite. "If the cats disturb you," she called over her shoulder, "just stick them in the basement. That's where they sleep at night."

The door slid shut, and in spite of Kirstie's instructions he sat in the recliner at the end of the hallway where he could watch for a while…just in case. Data rubbed against the leg of Gerard's chair, stared at him for a moment with those beautiful gold foil eyes, then leapt up onto the wide chair arm and settled himself, purring softly.

Gerard stifled a yawn. It was so tempting to lie back in the chair and take a nap himself, but his talk with Lawson and Kirstie, and his eagerness to see Megan later this afternoon, kept him awake. And now he had the keys. This couldn't be coincidence. Could it? This seemed more like an answer to prayer.

He yawned so deeply he dropped the keys, and Data jumped down.

Later. He could sleep later. After he had a long talk with Megan.

"You still like hot stuff, right?" Megan climbed into Gerard's car as he held the door for her after work. She had loaned her car to Carmen while Carmen's truck was in for repairs.

He looked askance at her. "Hot stuff?"

She glanced up at him. "You do, don't you?"

"What kind of hot stuff are you asking about?"

"Food, dummy." She grinned and reached to close the door. When he finally circled the car and slid behind the steering wheel, she said, "I can see spending the day with Kirstie knocked you off-kilter. Did she have one of her spells?"

"Nope, no spells, just stream-of-consciousness chatter."

Megan nodded as if she knew exactly what that meant. "I'm sure you discovered she can be quite the entertaining lady."

"She knows Springfield well and she guided me to your favorite restaurant. Unfortunately, it's not there anymore."

"No! The Hut? Lynley and I used to hang out there all the time during college."

He spread his hands. "There you have it. Long time ago."

Megan narrowed an eye. "You're older than me."

He chuckled as he switched on the engine and backed from his parking spot. "Will you need me to pick you up for work tomorrow?"

"No, Carmen's just running an errand to Monett. She'll leave my car at the clinic, so if you'll just drop me off there later I can get it."

"It'll be safe there then, I presume."

"This is Jolly Mill, not a scary section of Corpus Christi."

"Forgive me if that doesn't impress me the way it once did."

"There hasn't been a car theft in the history of Jolly Mill."

"Horse theft, maybe? I've read some history of the town. It goes back quite a ways. Any other criminal acts?"

"I'm only interested in attempted murder."

"We're still only working on one possible theory. Kirstie's suspicions may be wrong." He pulled from the parking lot onto the charming Victorian three-block main street of Jolly Mill. "Do you think her husband is capable of killing?"

There was a short silence, and Gerard glanced at Megan's silhouette, half in shadow as she watched out the side window. "Megan?"

"I don't think I'm the person to ask about that."

"Meaning you do."

She continued to stare at the buildings as the car moved past them. "I know too much about him, Gerard." Her voice softened, but it also gained an edge he hadn't heard in some time—not since he'd questioned her once before about her family. "I'm serious when I say that I'm biased. I dislike him. He's not just a weak man who can't stay away from women. He's also a fiend. I think he'd be capable of anything."

"I never met the man, but I trust your judgment."

Megan waved at several people on the sidewalk, and then she turned to Gerard. "No, you don't understand. I have a very personal reason to despise the man, and in this case my judgment can't be trusted."

As soon as Megan said the words she was sorry. Gerard was never one to back down from a challenge, and she'd just challenged him to question her. Maybe deep down she really did want him to ask her about it.

"And?" He wasn't demanding an answer. His voice was gentle, even encouraging.

"It's too personal."

"Megan, this is you and me here. We've talked about a whole lot of personal things. You can't be forgetting we broke down and cried in each other's arms when... After we had to deliver Daria from Joni's body."

Megan's eyes smarted with the tears that always burned her eyes when she was forced to think about that day. "Please, Gerard, don't."

"You can tell me anything. You can trust me with—"

"My life? I know." She closed her eyes and rubbed her forehead. *Get it over with. It's only the truth.* "My mother. She was...lonely a lot." Megan glanced through her eyelashes at Gerard, then back out past the buildings toward Capps Creek below the mill. "Dad was great, and he spent a lot of time with my brother, Jared, and me when he was home, but he traveled a lot, often overseas. Mom hated it, and it seemed like she resented us for having so much of Dad's attention when he was home."

"You've told me before you had a hit-and-miss home life."

"Yeah, well, Jared was always into cars and girls and didn't have a lot of time for his little sister. I think Mom was angry with me a lot."

"Why? Did she blame you for your father being gone?"

"No. I think she blamed me because he spent more time with his kids than he did with her, and she doted on Jared, so I was the only one left to be mad at." Megan knew she wouldn't even be sharing this private part of her mother's life if it hadn't also become a part of her own life. "Anyway, one day we had an all-school meeting in the gymnasium. Some visiting senator or something. I didn't feel well, so I skipped out and went home early. Dad was in Europe. Mom was supposed to be home alone. But I walked in on her with Barry, and they weren't playing Scrabble. They were in my bed."

The car slowed, speaking to Gerard's shock. "By saying 'with Barry' you mean—"

"The whole bit. The worst I could have imagined. My mother saw me and her eyes went all buggy. Barry saw me and I thought he was going to laugh out loud. From then on any time I saw him he gave me a knowing smile, almost as if he knew a secret about me instead of the opposite. He never said anything to me about it, and I made sure I was never alone with him because I didn't trust him not to touch me."

"Never a sign of remorse?"

"Never. He was a pervert. He had a rep, you know? Lynley and I had a classmate he seduced, and then she died."

"Does Kirstie know about this?"

"I never told her anything. I couldn't bring myself to do it. I think she was in denial for a long time. I mean, who wants to believe her husband's not only a player, but also possibly a killer? That's why she's finally beginning to suspect Barry. Lynley and I think he killed our classmate, Mara, because she was going to out him."

"What do you mean?"

"She was drunk, and she flat-out told Lynley he'd dumped her. The next morning she was dead. I think Kirstie's finally accepted that as the truth. It may be what she's working through right now with her blackouts. Lynley told her about Mara, even though I tried to convince her not to."

Gerard pulled to the side of the road and stopped. He brushed his fingers through the pale strands of his hair and leaned back against the headrest. "I need to meet him."

"Why? Do you think your cop genes will kick in and you'll be able to read guilt in his expression?"

Gerard shot her a humorless grin. "I could question him."

"You could try. Who besides Barry might have a reason

to hurt Kirstie? She's going to inherit a ton of money, apparently within two months if Lawson's doctors are guessing correctly."

"And yet he left her," Gerard said. "That's the mystery. He's taking a huge risk of being cut from the will."

"Kirstie and I can't figure that out either, except Kirstie can't bring herself to tell Lawson that Barry abandoned her. He could be banking on her tender heart."

"That's a huge risk for a man who wants that money. He's also risking that, if Kirstie dies, his daughter will contest the will. Poison is considered a woman's method of murder."

"I thought about that. It was a woman who poisoned Stud at Christmastime, but it was also a woman who tried to kill Tess last year in a speeding automobile," Megan said. "I don't think we can depend on statistics."

"How many women in Jolly Mill have been involved with Barry?" Gerard asked.

"I haven't been keeping track. What are you saying? You think he's seeing another woman who's decided she wants the inheritance money?"

"Kirstie told me he moved to Neosho to be closer to work. Do you think he's living with someone down there?"

"Lynley says no."

"Wishful thinking, or is she sure?"

"Lynley would make sure. Gerard, you've gotten to know her today, and you've met her friends. Any vibes there? You think one of the women connected to the clinic could possibly be poisoning Kirstie? Please tell me no. Those are my friends, and I can't imagine any of them hurting Kirstie."

"I don't know many people in Jolly Mill, but a sociopath is incapable of having compassion for anyone, even a woman as likeable as Kirstie, and you've described Barry as a sociopath."

Megan didn't want to hear that either. "This is Jolly Mill. It's hard to believe we might have a sociopath in this tiny town."

Gerard pulled back onto the road. "Don't retreat on me. This is still part of a fallen world, idyllic as it may be." He reached the end of Jolly Mill's main street and turned left onto the county road toward Megan's house. "It's estimated that four out of every hundred people are sociopaths. That doesn't mean they're killers, but it means they don't have normal compassion for other people. They are incapable of affection or conscience. If Barry is a sociopath and wants Lawson's money, he won't have the typical sociological—and certainly not spiritual—controls in place to keep him from doing what he feels needs to be done to get that money."

Megan shivered and crossed her arms. "I don't think I ever saw Barry show true affection for either his wife or his daughter unless he wanted something. Lynley complained about it when we were growing up."

"Then maybe you should seriously consider what the man could be capable of doing."

Megan closed her eyes for a moment. Oh, yes, she could do that. She had no trouble doing that. In fact, thinking about that hideous man's capabilities could make her past nightmares seem like swimming in Capps Creek.

TEN

Gerard watched Megan close her eyes and saw her face go pale. He knew what she was thinking. Murder was such a frightening word when it became personalized.

"What can be happening to Kirstie?" she whispered.

"We need to keep searching for answers. Kirstie's lab results should arrive within a couple of days."

She looked around them. "Gerard, where are we going?"

"Your place to eat, then because Lynley has a class tonight I thought we could come back into town and have a strategy session with Kirstie if she's awake by then. She was taking a nap when I left the house. I also want to have a look at the Lawson property."

"I forgot about Lynley's class. Kirstie's alone?"

"She was asleep."

"What if she wakes up disoriented?"

"Relax, Megan. Apparently she's never done that. She only has problems when she's tired. I made sure her doors were locked, and she told me she recently had the locks changed."

"Yes, but there's always a chance—"

"She usually has her blackouts in the evening, right?"

"Yes, and it's evening."

"But she's sleeping, and she told me she never wakes up from sleep into a blackout."

"I'm not sure about this."

"We'll check on her as soon as we eat." He wondered if there was something she took in the evening or before bed, some supplement they hadn't considered that might interact with the medicines she'd taken for the cancer she'd had two years ago. But Megan, Kirstie and Lynley were smart women, and they would have thought of those things already. Still… "You've checked all chemicals she works with, takes, et cetera?"

Megan nodded. "She, Lynley and I went through everything that goes into her mouth and checked for any possible drug or supplement interactions. She even stopped eating at local restaurants and started eating an organic, noninflammatory diet. We didn't find a thing."

"Contact lenses, toothpaste—"

Megan shook her head. "Kirstie wears glasses for reading. No contacts."

"Did you check for unexpected contaminants around the house she might be allergic to? Bug spray, termite treatment?"

"You mean something that would also poison Lynley and the cats? We've gone over all that. Everything we can think of." She sniffed and turned to look into the backseat. "Gerard, what are we going to eat? I don't see anything."

"I bought some salad and gluten-free pizza at a health food store Kirstie likes. It's in the back."

"Good. Forget the hot stuff. I'm starved."

He nodded and glanced at her. "Wait a minute. You already mentioned hot stuff. Is there a Mexican restaurant somewhere nearby? Because honestly, gluten-free pizza sounds like it should be against the law."

"Not if you're gluten intolerant."

"Which I'm not, and neither are you."

"But it's healthy food. The crust Kirstie gets is usually made out of cheese and cauliflower."

He grimaced. "I wish I'd asked before I bought it."

"Alec knew I liked hot stuff, and he told me about a Cajun restaurant in Monett. When we were dating he constantly tried to find something too hot for me to eat. I didn't meet my match until I went to Corpus Christi."

Gerard gently placed his tongue between his upper and lower teeth and concentrated on not biting down. How long had it been since he'd engaged in this type of imbecile emotional reaction—before today? Yes, he'd already betrayed his jealousy earlier this morning, but to be jealous about the simple fact that she had spoken with Alec about food? Unmanly.

Maybe it was because now that he'd met the guy, and because Kirstie had told him about how heartbroken Megan was after their post-graduation breakup—now, why had Kirstie thought it important to mention that?— he realized on several levels that despite a marriage contract, Alec may be interested in Megan as more than an employee. And right now Megan could be susceptible to the sweetheart of her youth, who didn't remind her of a recent murder every time she looked at him.

"Let me guess," he said, "you had a long talk with Alec about me."

"Really, Gerard. It doesn't always have to be about you." She grinned as she said it, but that didn't stop the sting of her words.

"But it was."

"Only parts of it. And no, he didn't get anything out of me about Kirstie or about why I'm here, though he tried. As did his mother. What on Earth prompted you to tell my friends how desperate I was to leave the mission?"

"I've found the truth is always best."

"But it only led to more questions. I wasn't lying, Gerard. I was keeping quiet about certain things. This was my secret and you violated it. All you've done is tempt my friends to pressure me harder to tell them something I don't plan to tell."

"Sorry. I'd hoped they would realize you've been through more than they can imagine and that they needed to give you some breathing space." Especially Alec. "But maybe it wouldn't hurt to share it with one or two of your closest friends."

"Not your decision to make."

"I'm simply advising, not making decisions."

"Well, stop talking to my friends about me, okay?"

"Fine." Gerard tapped the brake and made another left turn onto a farm road.

"Alec's willing to at least continue a discussion about your plans for Jolly Mill," Megan said.

"So you did talk to him about them?"

"I had the opportunity. I'm not sure he's ready to be your biggest ally in this venture, and if my friends find out why I'm really here and how dangerous that mission is, I could be your only ally in town, so it wouldn't hurt you to keep your mouth shut about the subject of Megan Bradley."

Gerard felt a lash of shame, not because of her words, but because right now he found himself caring less about the project than he did about Alec's proximity to Megan. Being here and meeting the man, seeing his resistance to the rehab plan, seeing Megan here on her home turf made Gerard feel like an outsider, when he had come here to help Megan through her PTSD and make inroads into helping the homeless who could be rehabilitated. He hadn't come here for a boxing match with her old boyfriend.

Megan pulled a wrapped cookie from her purse and held it out for him. "Nora made these, and I guarantee they're the best you've ever tasted." She unwrapped it, broke off a piece and held it to his lips. "Try it?"

He opened his mouth and allowed her to place it on his tongue, and the intimacy of that small act nearly made him miss the curve in the road. The combination of nuts and butter with a biscotti crunch nearly crossed his eyes. He groaned.

"Good, isn't it?" There was a grin in Megan's voice.

"Kind of heady for a starving man."

"Didn't you eat today?"

"Kirstie made me take her to a fancy teahouse south of Springfield for lunch."

"Uh-oh. Not enough food for a rancher, huh?"

"Let's just say my taste buds haven't been challenged enough."

"Then why not put the pizza in the freezer and head to The Bayou?" She rewrapped the cookie and put it back in her purse. "This'll be good for dessert. Alec implied the food at The Bayou will burn holes in our tongues if you request it hot."

Alec again. "He lives in Missouri. He doesn't know hot."

She dug into her pocket and pulled out a cell phone. "I'll call him for directions to the restaurant."

Gerard tapped the brake when he saw the end of her quarter-mile driveway. The next time he heard that man's name on Megan's lips, his head might explode. "You know what? That pizza's smelling better to me all the time. We can nuke that sucker and be chowing down in a few minutes. Why not just have a picnic on your porch swing?"

In the periphery of his vision he could see Megan studying him. "You seem just a tad grouchy."

No kidding. "Was it something I said?"

"The way you said it."

He turned onto the drive to her cabin in the woods. The Thompson cabin. "If you'll remember, I drove all night last night, I drove and walked and talked all day today, and I've had probably an hour of sleep tops since I got up yesterday morning."

"Who asked you to drive all night?"

"If you had answered my phone calls or replied to my messages I wouldn't have felt the need to—"

"Really?" She leaned forward to catch his gaze. "You're blaming me?"

"No, I'm just saying—"

"Somebody needs a nap." There was a hint of amusement in her voice.

He parked in front of the cabin and frowned at her. "You find that funny?" There was definitely a glimmer of suppressed humor in her eyes. Maybe even a glint of cheerfulness.

"I've never seen you jealous before."

He would not allow a blush to rise to his face. She was one woman who could undercut his confidence in a way no other woman had ever been able to do. He felt his frown turn to a scowl and he couldn't do anything about it. He couldn't argue with her because she was spot on. But if she was cheerful about it, that was a good thing, right?

Or maybe the thought of it was just laughable.

Nope. That couldn't be it. He knew better.

"I think you should go straight to bed as soon as you've eaten," she said.

"Yes, Mother. But what about Kirstie?"

Megan ignored him. "In fact, there's a luxuriously comfortable bed just inside those doors, and I can take a nice, long walk while you rest."

"If I go to sleep I could be out for ten hours. I've already unpacked my suitcase at Kirstie's." And there was no way he would chance compromising Megan's reputation by staying inside her cabin too long.

He got out of the car and opened the back hatch for the food. His eyes burned. Megan was right—he desperately needed rest, but he needed this time with Megan more.

"If you keep abusing your body like this," Megan said as she sprang from the car, "you won't be able to continue using brute force to keep the troublemakers out of the mission." She took the bag from him and preceded him up the porch steps and into the cottage. She didn't use a key.

"You didn't lock?" He did not believe this woman. After all she'd gone through, she didn't even consider the consequences of her lack of security?

She stopped and turned to give him a sheepish smile. "You had me distracted this morning."

"So you're blaming me?"

She shrugged. "You know that old saying? Turnabout's fair play. If you're going to blame me because you're sleepy—"

"Okay, got it." He reluctantly returned the smile and resisted the urge to tangle his fingers in her thick, ginger-colored hair and kiss her. It was something he'd wanted to do since he'd first seen her and spoken with her, heard her soft voice and seen the authentic compassion she showed to her patients, no matter how drunk or high they might be, how dirty, how smelly.

"Megan, we stopped by to visit Lawson Barnes."

"He's great, isn't he? Kirstie and her brother, Eugene, spent a lot of time with him when they were growing up. How was he?"

"If I didn't know he was sick, I wouldn't have guessed."

"I hate that all this happened to him." She unwrapped

the food and opened cabinets and drawers for eating plates and utensils. "He had a knack for people, and it wasn't a fake friendliness—it was genuine."

"I think that's why he was interested in the rehab project. If we do get it going here in Jolly Mill," Gerard continued, "the people who come here will be capable of learning new skills and contributing to the workforce. They will be upstanding members of society with families to feed and children to educate. They will not be killers."

Megan put ice in two tumblers, watching him askance. "But one out of every twenty-five people is a sociopath. You said so yourself. Do you have a foolproof test to cull out the bad ones?"

"Hans has a psychological screening that he uses for all upper management."

"That's not foolproof."

"Nothing in this life is foolproof. We can only do the best we know how to do."

"I know the rest of the line. We're supposed to trust God for the results."

"I didn't say that."

"You didn't have to."

He wanted to take her in his arms and promise her everything would be all right, but he'd learned long ago that was an empty promise. "You're still scared to death, aren't you?"

Her movements slowed as she stacked dinnerware on her tiny dining table. She looked up at him and swallowed. "What if you're bringing more danger here?"

"Trust me when I say that this won't be anything like the mission." He knew as he said the words that she wouldn't believe him because deep down, though she wouldn't even admit it to herself, she blamed him for the killer coming through the door.

She took a sharp breath and resumed setting the table. "Kirstie, of course, loves the whole idea."

He nodded.

Megan leaned over the pizza and inhaled. "Jalapeños!"

He eyed the room divider, behind which must be the bed. "Hottest I could find."

"I think this food needs to be heated the right way. Why don't you rest while I turn on the stove and get the cheese sizzling?"

He didn't need to be told twice. He stepped behind the red room divider, pulled off his shoes and sank onto the mattress. And he slept.

When he awakened it was dark outside. The faint fragrance of pizza continued to linger in the air. He got up and realized he was alone, that he was now ready to eat not only a healthy pizza, but also anything that came with it, including the grease-soaked cardboard box. He found more than half a pizza and a healthy helping of chopped salad waiting for him on Megan's tiny kitchenette table with a note telling him to rest as long as he wanted. She'd walked back to town to get her car and check on Kirstie.

Of course. Megan couldn't stop worrying about Kirstie. No matter how traumatized she was, how terrified she might be by what was taking place in Kirstie's life, Megan would not let Kirstie down. That was the reason she continued to blame herself for Joni's death. She'd have rather died herself than allow the life of another innocent to slip away. Megan Bradley was a true heroine.

ELEVEN

The first thing Kirstie Marshal noticed when she came to herself in the darkness was that something cold squished between her bare toes. She wiggled them. Mud?

The second thing she noticed was the fragrance of water, the whisper of it rushing through the night, the feel of moist air on her skin. She inhaled deeply the spring bouquet she loved so much.

She was standing barefoot outside, shivering, and she shouldn't be, not after the long nap she'd had this afternoon...or was that yesterday? What time was it? No watch. She'd taken it off when she took her nap so it wouldn't snag on the lace of her comforter.

As her eyes focused, she saw stars above and the moon near a horizon—though she couldn't tell which horizon.

A breeze kicked up, and her shivering increased. And then she panicked. Was she outside naked again? She reached for her thighs. No. Her fingers brushed against soft, thin material. Her nightgown. No robe, but at least this time maybe she wasn't going to give someone a free show the way she had a couple of weeks ago. If she recalled correctly, she was wearing the pink cotton gown last night...or tonight...or whenever she was last in her right mind.

"Hello?" she called out. "Anybody out there? Lynley?"

She listened for an answer, but heard only soft splashes nearby. The water she heard and smelled had to be from a large source; the drought had hit southwest Missouri hard this spring. Many of the creeks were drying up. The only water source large enough to be heard was Capps Creek. Her feet ached as she recalled waking with pain in her feet and then falling.

She'd obviously wandered away from home again, though her memory once again failed her. This time, she at least had her slippers on to keep the bandages from getting dirty. The last thing she remembered was sitting on the front porch watching the sun lower into the lace of the treetops as she settled her mind for bed.

Lynley wouldn't be home until late, and despite her misgivings, Kirstie had promised Gerard she would be fine alone. She never had these attacks like this, one right after the other. This was new. It frightened her.

"Lynley! Someone! Help me, please!"

She couldn't stop thinking about last night...or the night before—blast it all, what time was it?—when she'd sat outside stroking Data's silken fur and watching as Prissy and Poppy suddenly seemed interested in joining Data on her lap...

If I can remember that so clearly, I can't have Alzheimer's. How long have I been out here?

Kirstie examined the skyline and noted, as she watched the stars, that they seemed to be appearing one by one. The moon inched upward, not downward. At least she hadn't been up all night, judging by her lack of hunger or thirst.

A cat called to her from the darkness. As usual, they'd followed her. *I have to find a phone and call Gerard and Megan.* Too bad Kirstie's crazy half hadn't thought to at least leave a trail of breadcrumbs in her wake so she could figure out where she was. Maybe if she had dogs instead of cats, who might be trained to lead her back home...or maybe if she did as everyone suggested and used a cell phone...

Poor Lynley carried far too much weight on her shoulders. At thirty-two, she should be making a life for herself, not babysitting her mother with a questionable diagnosis of early-onset Alzheimer's, but at the same time, knowing Lynley loved her this much—to sacrifice everything for her—that gave her such a feeling of sweet peace and pride. The thought of actually being placed in a nursing facility terrified her.

Kirstie took a tentative step forward and realized her feet still hurt. Badly.

"Okay, Marshal, how far have you wandered this time?" For some crazy reason, the sound of her own firm voice comforted her. She didn't sound crazy. "Thank goodness for the slippers...and the gown."

She stretched her arms out wide to better explore her surroundings and did a more complete study of what horizons she could see through the trees.

There. West. The palest shading changed the dark gray to black as the sun moved farther from the horizon.

It was only going to get darker, and despite this clearing in the forest she wouldn't be able to depend on the moon to illumine her way; no reflection of that light reached this deeply into the shadow of the hillside. Unaccustomed to waiting, Kirstie crept slowly through the woods, making her way east because the last time she'd gone west and had fallen into the mill pond. A cat brushed against her legs, and then another.

Twigs crunched beneath the soles of her slippers, hurting her feet. A flash of light startled her. For a moment, she was convinced the light was simply a new symptom of her illness—her poisoning—and she would need to have her eyes checked. But as she turned to glance up the hill-side, she saw the round glow of a flashlight and the bare, familiar outline of Uncle Lawson's resort in the reflection of that light.

Strange. Why would anyone use a flashlight when the electricity was on at the resort?

But if it was Gerard, he wouldn't know about the circular dimmer switches. He must be looking for her. "Thank you, Jesus," she whispered, then, more loudly, called, "Hello? I'm down here."

The light disappeared. She turned to look behind her. Perhaps the light had been a reflection? But she saw no one.

She stopped for a moment and listened. She couldn't just wait here all night. She'd given the keys to Gerard, so he, and probably Megan, must be up in the main building. It had to be them. No one else would have reason to be there. The electricity must be off again. They'd had trouble with that last year, and she'd planned to bring in an electrician to repair everything at once.

"Megan?" she called. "Gerard? It's me, Kirstie. Hold on a minute, would you?"

The light that had been burning steadily a moment ago was nowhere to be seen.

"Hey, guys! Gerard, Megan? We're down here, cats and all. Wait for us!"

She tripped over one of the cats in her rush to reach them. Obviously her voice wasn't carrying up the hill. Despite the pain in her feet, she picked herself up and ran, recalling Lynley's assurance to the others that her mother would not rest long enough to allow her feet to heal quickly.

Well, of course not.

Grasping branches and tree trunks, searching with her toes for the softest places on the forest floor, she made her way up the rocky slope, using memory to help her avoid some of the boulders she knew were nearby. She ignored the pain in her feet. She'd fostered this form of intentional ignorance in the past four months. Ignoring the burden of the diagnosis made by a doctor who wouldn't even attempt to discuss other options with her, she had rejected his opinion, and the second opinion of his respected colleague.

Doing so had helped lately. When she had control of her mind, she had excellent overall control. The only things she could not remember were what happened during her memory lapses. And so when she recovered from one, she simply reconnected with the activities she'd been involved in before the lapse.

How many times had she told anyone who would listen that this was not Alzheimer's?

Did she have sundowner's syndrome right now? No. She'd successfully found her bearings. In the dark, no less. She had worked with Alzheimer's patients when she still had her nursing job at the clinic, and she knew the signs.

Sure, she had memory lapses. It was what happened to women her age. They got wiser and more alluring but they forgot things. At her annual pajama weekend with Nora, Carmen and others, she'd noticed how, each year, they had to help each other more often to think of a particular word.

Okay, maybe she did have a little more trouble with memory than Rosie or Linda…and maybe even Nora… but Cathy fought the battle just as hard. Carmen wasn't there yet, but she hadn't even begun menopause.

Thank goodness for Megan and Gerard.

Kirstie was about to release another branch and step forward when a whisper of confusion sifted through the air around her. She stopped and closed her eyes. No. Not now. Not again so soon!

Always, the confusion.

She took the step, and a wisp of a limb slapped her in the face. She gasped and stumbled backward, suddenly afraid.

First the confusion, and then the fear. It was a familiar fear, and she only recognized it when it hit her again... danger in Jolly Mill. She was convinced of it.

Danger for her? Maybe for others? But why? The ring...

That was it. A ring. She could close her eyes and see that ring, and it was familiar. She could also see the hand that wore it, big and strong—a little too heavy. It was a man's ring, and she knew the man. She saw his face. He'd been gone a long time. She had to try to remember this. Had to remember.

It was Eaton Thompson. She caught a flash of his face—a young face, sixteen, but he was big even then. She dated him when he first came to town their junior year of high school, but after two dates with him he expected payment for the dinners and movies. She'd given him forty dollars and told him not to come around again.

The memory faded and Kirstie's next thought went to Lynley. Fear trounced on her in earnest.

She shook her head, trying to retain her focus this time. Kirstie had to get home and contact Lynley. No time to give in to this black spirit.

"Megan Bradley, don't leave me out here in the dark!" she cried toward the resort. "Megan!" Her cry turned to a scream.

The circle of darkness continued its deliberate march until she had forgotten again. All was gone except for the fear, and she ran up the hill, stumbled on some stones and felt herself falling.

Someone caught her. Warm hands, soft voices. More than one. Something about those voices calmed her fear. She stopped trying to run and allowed those gentle hands to direct her. She felt caught in a dream. The darkness tried to take the voices from her with its roaring sound of thunder, but she fought it back and sought the sound of those voices. Even if she couldn't see them, as long as she heard them she would be okay.

Megan helped Lynley ease Kirstie's pliable form onto a mossy boulder and then pulled out her cell phone, pushing Data's inquisitive nose away. "I'm calling Gerard."

"Just help me first." Lynley held the flashlight out to Megan. "Hold this." She placed her hands on Kirstie's cheeks. "Mom? Mom, listen to me!" She looked up at Megan. "This is crazy. So soon after the last one? What if she's having strokes of some kind?"

"Nothing on the CT scan. I read it myself and I had two of my best radiologists read it. Clean."

Lynley patted her mother's face again, tenderly brushing the hair from her forehead. "What I don't get is why she was calling *your* name."

"I thought you were in class tonight. I'm sure she did too."

"It's a good thing I wasn't or I'd still be an hour away."

"Why did you come home?" Megan watched her friend's grim expression in the glow of the flashlight.

"I called the house."

"Just to check?"

Lynley nodded. "No one answered. Mom always answers. She never leaves it for the machine."

Megan looked up the hill. All was dark now. "I thought I saw some kind of light flashing up at the resort a few minutes ago. I thought maybe Kirstie had decided to make a quick check to ensure Gerard got a good impression when he saw it."

"I didn't see any light. When the lights at the lodge are on they're like beacons."

"It was more like a flashlight."

"I need to call Gerard. Now." Megan punched Gerard's speed dial.

"She's wandering somewhere," Lynley said.

Megan realized Kirstie was staring as if mesmerized straight into the glow of the flashlight, and she aimed it away as Gerard answered.

"You left me sleeping in your bed?" came his deep voice almost immediately. "Are you nuts? What if someone had come to visit? What kind of a reputation do you think that would have given—"

"Yes, Mother. Listen, Kirstie's having one of her episodes right now and we need your help"

"How's she behaving?"

Megan studied Kirstie's pretty, wide-open eyes, her fidgeting hands, the fear that flashed into her expression whenever she looked at Lynley. "I don't know, but she's wide-awake, she's just not here with us."

"Mom, what's going on right now?" Lynley asked softly.

"How can I find you?" Gerard asked.

"Just downhill from the resort, out on the open hillside."

"I'm pulling up to Kirstie's house. Can I drive there?"

"You can get here faster by foot. The main entrance is on the other side of the section and the gates to the side roads have been bolted shut to keep out trespassers. Do you have a flashlight? You're going to need it. Even with it you can get lost."

"Have a little faith. I've seen it from the road in the daylight."

"There may be someone up at the lodge."

"Be there in a few." He disconnected.

"I'm glad it's not raining," Lynley said. "Help me get her up. Let's try to lead her back to the house. Did you notice how she keeps looking toward you?"

"Nope." Megan reached down and grasped Kirstie's arm. "Kirstie, let's get home. I bet your feet are hurting."

Kirstie blinked and made eye contact with Megan for a fraction of a second, then nodded.

"See that?" Lynley said. "She'll look at you. It's like she's scared to even look at me. When she hears you talking she calms down. I think I'm just making her more nervous. What's up with that?"

"It's called a mother's love. Would you relax? Our main focus needs to be keeping her calm. We both need to keep talking."

"You talk," Lynley snapped. "She gets more agitated with me."

"You're the one who's agitated. Calm yourself." Megan tugged gently on Kirstie's arm, and she got up. "Let's go back to the house, okay, Kirstie?"

Megan glanced at Lynley, who watched her with an expression that was all too familiar, though it had been many years since Megan had seen it or even thought about it. Jealousy.

Megan and Lynley had been best friends since kindergarten, enjoying sleepovers at both their homes at least once a week. During sixth grade, however, Megan spent less and less time at home and started going home with Lynley more often after school. Barry was never home, anyway, so it was just the three of them.

Kirstie had always accepted her with warmth and laughter and attention, and Megan soaked it in like a flower bathed in spring sunshine. Those were the times

Megan picked up on Lynley's withdrawal. But they were children then. Why was Lynley behaving like a child again?

"Let's take it slowly." Megan shone the light at the ground.

"Is Gerard on the way?" Lynley asked.

"He should be here any time." Megan took Kirstie's hand. "Kirstie, can you hear me? Do you know where we are?"

Kirstie looked at Megan and stumbled.

"Would you be careful?" Lynley glared at her through the dim light. "You know, you never have given anybody a good enough explanation for leaving your job in Texas."

"Not now, please. We have more important things to consider."

"Three months left, and you risk all kinds of grief so you can run back home and take care of Mom? Almost as if she's your own mother, and I don't have what it takes to help her."

"I came to help you too, idiot. Kirstie hated to think you would turn your back on the career of your heart to do a job anyone could do just as easily."

"Someone like you?"

"That's not what I—"

"You were closer to her than to your own mom." Lynley's narrowed gaze sliced across Megan's face, and Megan saw pain in her eyes. Once again, the result of lifelong emotional abandonment by her father.

"I wasn't closer to her than you were," Megan reminded her friend. "Kirstie was good at mothering others, but you were her own beloved child. Nothing came before that. Nothing comes before that now. Believe me. I have no doubt of that."

Lynley's gaze shifted away, and Megan stopped breathing for a moment at the latent resentment resting there. The pain of it plunged deeply.

"I'm not trying to interfere in your relationship with Kirstie," Megan said. "You should know me better than that."

"I asked why you came back," Lynley said. "Here. To *my* mother instead of yours. It's like you've shut me out these past three weeks."

Oh, Lynley. No. "I thought you understood about my relationship with my mother."

"But here you are, all grown up, and you still can't get along with her?"

"I choose not to accept the verbal jabs." There'd been too many already. "The best memories I have are of those six weeks when Dad went overseas for work and she went with him."

"I remember. They left you with us." There was a darkness in Lynley's voice, an edge that cut through Megan. This wasn't real. "You were always 'poor little Megan. That precious child. So smart. So good at everything, and no one is taking the time to teach her things she needs to know.'"

Megan swallowed, glancing down at Kirstie's hands, which Kirstie had begun to wring in obvious agitation. "Lynley, would you keep your voice down? What's wrong with you? This isn't like you at all."

"Stop telling me what to do."

Megan focused on controlling her own irritation. She leaned closer to Kirstie. "Time to come with us now, Kirstie. Can you answer us?"

"I'm trying," Kirstie's reply startled Megan. "But there's danger. Such danger. I didn't know. Couldn't know. We can't tell, Megan. Remember, nothing. Shh."

Lynley gasped. "Megan mustn't tell?" She released her mother and took a step back. "What's this about?"

Megan put her fingers to her lips. "She may be coming around."

"Good, then maybe she can tell me why you two have been keeping secrets from me."

Megan wanted to slap her hand across Lynley's mouth to shut her up. And yet there was something going on with her. "Lynley, stop and think about what you're saying. This isn't you talking. Something's going on."

"Just because your boyfriend's a cop doesn't mean you suddenly earned the right to control all our lives."

"I have no intention of coming between you and Kirstie."

"And yet you have."

"No, I haven't. You aren't seeing things as they really are right now." Megan glanced down the hill. Where was Gerard? "You're the most important person in the world to her. You're the sister I never had."

"But you still can't trust me with your secrets?"

"You don't understand, and right now isn't the time—"

"Who are you to tell me what is and isn't the time to know why my mother is having these spells? You suspect something else?" Lynley studied her mother's face once more, stepped over to her and pressed fingers gently against Kirstie's shoulders. "You suspect..." She turned and stalked back to Megan, face inches away. "You suspect me?" Her voice rose in outrage.

"Of course not, Lynley. You're really losing control."

Lynley's eyes widened. She raised her hand and drew back.

Megan winced even as she watched the tears form in her friend's eyes and the hand draw away. She might as well have followed through with the slap. Megan felt as if the world was cracking apart, as if the sisterhood she'd always shared with Lynley was the jealous, harsh, ugly kind of sibling rivalry and had carried into adulthood.

Megan knew better, yet she felt her own emotions subverting her logic.

How could Lynley talk to her like this? Yes, she most likely had a sociopath for a father, but her mother had overcompensated to make up for that, had at times smothered Lynley with her desire to protect and encourage. And if some of that tendency had encompassed Megan, who'd needed that warmth so badly, why did Lynley feel as if she, alone, should have received every drop? Wasn't the abundant love of her own flesh-and-blood mother enough for her?

"I'm sorry." Megan fought her own anger at the battle she saw taking place in Lynley's eyes. "Sorry I ever visited you, ate at your family's table, helped your mother clean the kitchen, do the dishes. I'm so sorry that while you sat in your room and read and talked on the phone to your other friends—all your other friends—that I stayed and helped your mother with chores you didn't want to do. So we had a friendship. So what? Couldn't you even allow me that?"

Lynley turned away. "I never wanted a sister. I wanted a father. Did it ever occur to you that my father went out at night because he didn't like company around all the time?"

Megan bit her lip. Lynley's bitterness was so contagious. "You know what? Kirstie needs us. If you want to have a slap fight, I'll be glad to schedule a time for it later, but right now start thinking about someone besides yourself."

"Stop it." The voice, deep and trembling, came from Kirstie, as if forced through deep water.

Megan and Lynley turned to her. Lynley grasped her mother's hands. "Mom?"

TWELVE

For a moment, Kirstie couldn't move. It was as if she had to fight her way from beneath a hot tub of sand. She could almost convince herself the argument that dragged her back to reality was part of the blackout, but she knew better. Why were her girls fighting?

She blinked up at Megan and Lynley, surrounded by darkness, and then as suddenly, as if she had never gone to that other place of terror and darkness, she saw their faces clearly in the glow of the flashlight. She'd been thrust into the role of referee. How long had it been since she'd had to do that? Since they were eight?

"What are you girls fighting about?"

"Mom, where did you go?" Lynley asked. "Why were you so—"

Kirstie clasped Lynley's hands and squeezed gently, kissed her daughter's fingertips as she had when Megan and Lynley were little, and patted her face. "Sweetheart, nothing for you to worry about."

"But Megan knows."

"How can she? I don't even know."

Lynley pulled away from Kirstie's touch. "That's all I needed to hear." She shot a look at Megan that was a few degrees colder than outer space, then pivoted away and strode down the dark hillside, her slender shoulders stiff.

Perhaps she meant for Megan and Kirstie to follow, but she would have to cool off on her own this time. "I've spoiled her, I'm afraid."

Megan helped Kirstie sit back on the ground, then joined her. Immediately, they were surrounded by cats. "I don't think that's it. Let's wait for Gerard. He can carry you down and save your pretty feet."

"Thank you, my dear." Kirstie patted Megan's arm. "And thank the Lord I've at least got clothes on this time. I don't think poor Elmer Batschelet will ever recover from that one night..." She sighed. This whole thing was so humiliating. "Anyway, my feet are killing me, and it seems my wounded child is feeling the pain."

"She knows we're keeping something from her."

"I'm sure she does. In time I'll tell her all about it, but not yet. If she knew I suspected poison it would no longer be a secret. She'd go off half-cocked, ready to shoot the first suspect—meaning her father—no questions asked. You know how she is. I'm just sorry it's causing a rift between the two of you."

"We've had plenty of rifts."

"This one's different, though, isn't it?"

For a moment there was silence. "Yeah. It is."

"Can you tell me how?"

"She's never hated me before."

Kirstie reached up and smoothed a curl of amber hair from Megan's chin. "She doesn't hate you now, sweetheart. I can assure you of that."

Megan gave a watery sniff and then straightened her shoulders. "Have you remembered any more?"

"I think so, but it's like a dream that goes away as soon as I wake up." She rubbed her face, aggravated with herself. "The circle isn't as big as I'd thought. Not big at all. And there's more than just a circle, but I can't quite make the memory come back. It's like a clue. It's something I can't stop thinking about, but it's fuzzy, you know?"

"Oh, Kirstie, this is so frustrating."

"Were you and Gerard up there?" Kirstie nodded up the hill toward the building.

"No. I left Gerard at the cottage sleeping and walked back to the clinic to get my car. He was so tired he didn't even eat before he was deep asleep. I didn't have the heart to wake him." Megan shook her head. "Alpha males and their god complexes. Think their bodies are immortal. No matter how much you try to tell them—"

"Megan."

"Yes?"

"You're telling me no one with a key has been up there?"

"I thought I saw a flicker of light up that way when Lynley and I were looking for you, so I thought it might be you. Don't you have two sets of keys?"

"I don't have them on me."

"Are you sure? Maybe you left a set up there? We heard you shouting my name. Lynley freaked over it."

Kirstie sighed. "Sorry about that. I never wanted to mess with your friendship with Lynley. When you two were little, if I showed you the tiniest bit more attention than I showed her, she let me know about it. I'd have thought she'd do the same to you."

"I remember, but she's grown now."

"Old family dynamics are difficult to overcome. Isn't that why you avoid visiting your family?"

"Probably."

"We need to call Sheriff Moritz," Kirstie said.

"Why?"

"He needs to check out the resort. We might have had vandals."

Megan forced back a chill. "You were shouting pretty loudly. I'm sure if anyone was there, they got out in a hurry. Besides, Gerard's on his way up to us now, and he needs to see the place anyway. Why don't we wait until he gets here and then he and I can check it out after we get you back to the house?"

"No. Not you, Megan. If someone's trespassing—"

"Then we can call the sheriff. Gerard can handle anything, believe me. Besides, I doubt you'd be able to talk him out of it once I mention it to him, which I will do if Lynley doesn't beat me to it. You wanted us to protect you. This is part of the job."

Kirstie didn't want that. Not at all. But she'd been the one to drag poor Megan into this. "Fine. But I hate this."

"Who doesn't?"

"Nora called me this afternoon, and we had a long talk. She's convinced me to eliminate Barry's presence from the house completely. She's been bugging me about it for weeks. She's also begging me to move in with her for a while. She even wants to hire a housekeeper. Did she tell you that?"

"Yes."

"You haven't told her I suspect poisoning, have you?" Kirstie asked.

"I haven't told anyone anything you wanted kept silent. She may have jumped to her own conclusions. If you suspected it, what's to keep her from thinking the same? Why don't you accept her invitation?"

"What, move?"

"At least for a while."

"Look, I've agreed to redo the master suite, okay? I'm

starting tomorrow. It'll keep my mind occupied and get Barry's presence out of the house."

"You're not supposed to drive right now. Is Nora taking you shopping?"

"Nope. Gerard." He didn't know it yet, of course, but since Kirstie had chosen him as her bodyguard, and since she trusted him, she was putting him to good use. "I'm going to have him drive me to town to buy paint and talk to a flooring company. I'm going to rip out the carpet in the master bedroom that Barry always loved so much and put in wood floors."

"You always loved white pine."

Kirstie grinned. Megan knew her well. "That's right. And I'm going to paint the whole suite the colors of sand and seashells and surf. Maybe a sunset or two."

"Why limit the change to the master suite? Why not change out the whole house? It's yours, Kirstie. Make it what you want it to be."

"I can't focus long enough right now. I'll start with the suite and work my way up to the tougher decisions."

"Sounds good, but hire someone to do it. You don't need paint fumes to add to anything else that could be affecting you." Megan touched Kirstie's arm. "While you're at it, you also might consider Lynley's health. I know you're worried about her, but have you considered she may be affected by whatever's poisoning you?"

At that calm statement, Kirstie felt as if she'd been slammed by a sledgehammer. "Why?"

"Can't you tell Lynley isn't behaving like herself? She's a grown woman, and tonight she suddenly started behaving like a spoiled little girl. That's not like her, even factoring in the old family dynamics."

"But she's been emotional lately. The divorce plus my illness have knocked her to her knees."

"She nearly slapped me just before you woke up. She hasn't done that since we were in first grade and I told the teacher on her for tricking the other kids into eating dirt."

"Ah, yes, the special supplement she told everyone had all kinds of wholesome minerals in it."

"Will you at least consider staying with Nora? If you and Lynley are being poisoned by something in the house, staying away for a few days would prove it."

Kirstie put a hand out and grasped Megan's wrist. "Tell me that shadow coming toward us is Gerard."

"It is."

"Good. I thought it was a tree walking up the hill. I'm not in the mood for another one of my episodes tonight."

"You realize you can't be left alone again."

"I know. And you're right. I have even more reason to find my killer now."

Megan caught her breath audibly. "I wish you wouldn't put it that way. You can't have a killer unless you're dead, and you aren't. At least stay a few days with Nora, both you and Lynley."

"If you and Gerard can get me safely back to the house, I'll have a talk with Lynley and I'll call Nora." Kirstie hadn't considered the possibility that her stubbornness could be placing her daughter in danger too.

Much as they both loved Nora, that dear woman could be intrusive and bossy if they allowed it, but what Megan said made sense. Staying with Nora would be a lot better than being locked up in an Alzheimer's unit.

Lynley was seated on the carpeted staircase with her hands covering her face, hair tangled around her slumped shoulders. Megan walked in and held the door for Gerard to carry Kirstie inside. When Lynley looked up it was obvious she'd been crying.

"All's well," Megan said softly.

Gerard placed Kirstie on her feet, and she thanked him and gestured for him to follow her into the kitchen. "At least have something warm to drink before you head out again. Did you get to eat that delicious pizza?" She and Gerard left Megan and Lynley alone. Kirstie had always been thoughtful that way.

Lynley looked back down at her feet. "I can't believe what happened up there a while ago."

"What part?"

"The part about me almost hitting you. There's no way to make up for what I said. I don't know what came over me. It was like...you know...what I've always heard menopause is like."

"PMS maybe?"

Lynley shook her head.

"I didn't think so." And it frightened Megan. Poison, maybe?

Kirstie and Gerard were chattering comfortably in the kitchen, so Megan went up the stairs and sank down on the step below Lynley. "Look, I know you're in desperate need of some answers. So am I. Kirstie wants Gerard here to help take a load off your shoulders, and I'm here to help, not come between you and your mother."

Lynley covered her face again. "That wasn't me, Megan. Really. It was a feral hog pretending to be me. I'm so sorry."

"No apologies, okay? I don't have all the answers you want, but I can give you one answer if you'll promise, promise not to tell anyone, especially Kirstie. Not now. Not until I tell you it's okay. And it may never be okay."

Lynley slowly raised her head. Her dark eyes held Megan's. Was this the right thing to do? Would this be too much for her to handle?

But Lynley was strong, and Megan had begun to realize Gerard was right about sharing the emotional load. If she wanted to recover, she had to get some of this out of her system.

"I've been avoiding Gerard since I came back from Corpus Christi."

Lynley raised her eyebrows as if to say, "Tell me a piece of information I don't know."

"I think you've been picking up on it, and I know we've always told each other everything, so you've felt left out."

"It's not my feelings I'm worried about right now." Lynley's hair fell back into her face, and in an impatient gesture she gathered it all up together and tied it into a knot in the back. "Spill."

"You've had some pretty gnarly experiences in the E.R. We've compared notes."

"And I've always won the contest for blood and gore."

Megan felt a catch in her throat. "Not this time."

Lynley's eyes darkened. She leaned forward and put a gentle hand on Megan's shoulder. "What happened, honey?"

"I had a pregnant patient who was living with her sister at the mission. Her name was Joni, and she was still in her teens, ready to go into labor any day. I was examining her in a curtained cubicle of the clinic when I heard the sound of ripping and looked up to find a knife slicing the curtain and the smiling face of a stinking man in his forties."

Lynley's hand tightened on Megan's shoulder, and Megan placed her own hand over it, needing the human contact. "Before I could reach for the gun in my pocket, he'd plunged through the curtain and shoved his knife deeply into my patient's heart."

When Megan looked up, she saw that she had Lynley's

wide-eyed attention. The horror in her friend's face was tangible. "I'm sorry. Maybe you don't need to—"

"Stop that, Megan. What happened?"

"I shot him, but the damage was done. I'd been carrying a weapon since Gerard bought it for me for self-defense. I'd carried it when I accompanied his sister, Tess, on trips when she was being stalked last year."

"You did mention your clinic in Corpus Christi wasn't your dream job. What else did you do?"

"What I didn't do was shoot him in time, and that will always haunt me. He fell over my patient's body, and I had to shove him off her before Gerard got there and I could deliver the baby."

Finally, Lynley's face paled. "You had to perform a postmortem C-section."

Megan didn't realize tears were pouring down her face until she gave a watery sniff and Lynley pulled a tissue from her pocket and dabbed at Megan's nose and cheeks, then handed her the tissue to do her own mopping.

"Gerard?" Lynley asked. Her own voice quivered.

"He worked right beside me. He was the first one to hold the little girl, Daria, and he was the one who found our patient's sister and broke the news to her while I cleaned up. Tess and Sean, her fiancé, called the police and helped us with the fallout."

Lynley sniffed. "Oh, honey, I wish you had told me. I wish I could've been there for you."

Megan felt her whole body shake with sobs she'd never given way to. When Lynley's arms opened for her, she laid her head against Lynley's shoulder and wept.

"Yeah, I know," Lynley whispered. "It was my worst nightmare for you."

"How could you know?"

"You worked with the most damaged of souls. You

brought them back to life over and over again. That girl who died? She probably didn't even know the father of her baby."

Megan shook her head. "She had an older sister who tried to do right by her, but how does a sister teach a younger sister how to behave in polite society when neither of them lived in polite society?"

"Who has little Daria now?"

"The older sister, Mamie. A family in one of the churches that supports the mission has taken them in."

"So that's why you wouldn't stay here with us when you came to town. You were having nightmares and screaming."

"How'd you know that?"

"Because you've always had nightmares. And you avoided Gerard because he reminded you too much of what happened."

"He wants me to get counseling."

"He's right. But you're obviously not avoiding him now."

"How can I? We need him."

"Yeah, I have to admit I'm more comfortable with him staying upstairs."

"I always felt safe with him until Joni's murder."

Lynley patted Megan's shoulder and handed her another tissue. "Mop up your face."

Megan did as she was told. "We're going up to the lodge tonight. I saw a light, and it wasn't Kirstie. She saw it too."

"Why don't you stay here and let Gerard and Moritz check it out?"

"Because I need to do this."

"You're not a cop."

"My job at the mission was to protect lives. I failed Joni. If someone's up at the lodge, then I need to know why they're there and if they have anything to do with what's going on with Kirstie."

Lynley gave her a half-smile. "I had a long talk with myself on my way back down the hill. I could have kicked myself. I've always been Mom's only child, and she goes out of her way to protect me. You, though, are her hero. She always admired you and trusted you to keep me out of trouble when we were together. She's still doing that, and so are you. That's why there are still secrets. Am I right?"

"If I answered that, would there still be secrets?"

"I'll get it out of you eventually, you know."

"Everything will come out soon, I think. But first, a routine check of the lodge is in order." Megan gave Lynley a hug and went in search of Gerard. They had work to do, and she needed to talk to him.

THIRTEEN

"I can do this alone." Gerard watched Megan duck into the passenger side of her car parked in Kirstie's driveway.

"You've never even been to Barnes Lodge and Resort, much less seen the inside." She reached into her glove compartment and came out with her Smith & Wesson .357 Magnum.

"I know how to find my way around an unfamiliar building in search of dangerous people, but my job would be easier if I didn't have a sidekick to protect."

"You know arguing won't do you any good," she said as she checked the seven-chamber cylinder.

"Yet I still do it because someday I think you might listen."

She pulled a tiny flashlight from the console. "What do you think that says about you?"

"Maybe I keep expecting you to use common sense." He wanted to add *for once,* but that was unfair. She typically used a great deal of sense. She'd just lost sight of it since Joni's death.

She flipped on the powerful little light and shone it up from her chin, placing the intriguing lines of her face into shades of gray, white and black as she made a face at him, obviously unaware that her nose was red from crying.

She then closed the car door and turned toward the woods beside the house. "Let's go see if there are bogeymen at the resort."

He followed close behind and switched on his own light. "I see you and Lynley made up quickly."

"Force of habit. Any time we fought when we were kids, Kirstie made us hug each other and apologize immediately. We just haven't fought like that since we were kids."

"Why now?"

"Good question. She's onto us already, Gerard. Kirstie was calling my name when we found her and Lynley threw a jealous fit. It was enough to make me wonder if Lynley hasn't somehow been affected by whatever's causing Kirstie's blackouts." There was a pause. "Actually, I wasn't much better myself. I offered to set up a slap fight for later."

Gerard bit his tongue to keep from laughing, but concern sobered him quickly enough. "Do you think we should leave them alone at the house if they're both affected?"

"Good try," Megan said with a glance over her shoulder, "but I think I've convinced Kirstie to stay at Nora's for a while. Where she goes, Lynley will go. Nora's coming over in a few minutes. Kirstie's going to have work done on the house, and I'm going to suggest she and Lynley buy new clothing, shoes, toiletries, everything before they go to Nora's."

"Now you're thinking like a cop."

"I've been around you too long."

Gerard disagreed. He didn't think she'd been around him nearly long enough. "Anyway, good job."

"We'll see what she says once she's thought about it."

Megan kicked her pace into high gear and Gerard followed, admiring her speed.

She reminded him of Kirstie. "You had a good mother substitute."

Megan looked around at him. "Kirstie? Yeah. Kind of strange, though, don't you think? She took my mother's place in my life after her husband took my father's place in bed?"

"Kirstie doesn't know about that?"

"I'm not like Lynley. I don't tell all I know, and I think Kirstie knows enough already, so why load her down with more? Anyway, is it necessary for us to get into this conversation while we could be stalking a perp in the darkness through a haunted lodge?"

"No such things as haunted lodges if you pray over them right," Gerard said.

"Then maybe it isn't haunted because Lawson Barnes is a praying man, but there were lights up there earlier, and you apparently have the only keys in town. Did I tell you I threatened to give away my mother's dirty little secret if she didn't stop seeing Barry?"

"And yet you didn't give her away?"

"She told me she would never see him again. I believed her. She was pretty broken up about it." Megan paused. "At least she pretended to be."

"Do you know if she ever saw other men?"

"I don't think so. You didn't see her expression when I walked in on them. It was as if her world had just exploded."

"What about your world?"

"I was angry."

"You've never forgiven her for it?" Gerard asked.

"I think I was angrier with Barry. You'd have to know my mother. She struggled with depression off and on, and

I felt Barry took advantage of that. Sometimes I wonder if I'm to blame for Barry Marshal still getting away with wicked activities. I often wish I'd spoken up."

"But that would have made everything more real."

Megan's footsteps slowed. She glanced over her shoulder at him. "What's this special gift you have of knowing what's on my mind? And don't tell me it's because I'm so readable."

"No, that's not it."

"I guess I could say my mother did me a favor because the memory of finding her and Barry like that stuck with me through my teens and kept me chaste in the face of Alec's demands."

Gerard wanted to shoot his fist into the air and cheer. "I'm glad something good came out of it."

"But if Barry's somehow poisoning his family in order to get Lawson's money for himself, then I could be partially to blame for what's happening to them now. Maybe Kirstie would have kicked him out years ago if I'd told her."

Gerard hated the sound of anxiety in her voice. "You think someone living with a childhood trauma should be blamed for the actions of another person? He was the reason for your trauma, Megan. You're not the reason for what's happening now, and I doubt any word from you could have been a revelation for her."

"You think she knew?"

"I think she knew a lot, and you weren't the cause of the lifelong pain of her marriage. You were a child."

A moment later, Megan aimed her light up the hillside to reveal the lodge-style front of the resort. "There it is." Megan led him between two looming buildings to the front of the huge double doors that were the lodge entrance. She turned to Gerard, and a half-smile touched her face in the shadows of the porch roof. "Thank you."

"Welcome. And since you're opening up about that, how do you feel about yet one more subject?"

Her smile died.

"I just want to make one point, Megan."

She sighed. "Okay, I can see you're going to start spewing steam from your ears if you can't have your say."

"I'm glad you told Lynley about Joni. I wish you'd keep talking about it, telling more friends, sharing the load. It's what friends are for. Another reason I drove here last night was because I couldn't get Evelyn Murphy off my mind. Remember her?"

"How could I forget? She had compartment syndrome. She lost her leg."

"And you explained how that happened. Her blood supply was cut off from her leg. Ever since you left I've thought about her, even dreamed about her."

"After Joni's murder and Stud's death at Christmas and your own sister being stalked and almost killed, you're thinking about a case from last year?"

"I'm pointing out that it's exactly what you could be doing to yourself emotionally and spiritually if you don't ask for help."

"You think I should find a therapist."

"Most definitely. You can't keep that bottled up inside and expect to heal from it. You're a doctor. You know better."

"But I need time."

"You don't have time. Evelyn didn't have time, remember? It was tragic, especially because it was preventable. You said so yourself."

Megan shook her head. "This isn't the same thing."

"You're shutting yourself away from your main source

of help. You were getting to know Him again after all these years."

"I can't go there yet, Gerard."

"He's your spiritual strength."

She shook her head. "That blood supply you're so sold on was poisoning me." There was a tremble in her voice he hadn't heard before. "It's hot in Texas in more ways than one. I can't do everything God expects me to do."

"He only expects you to lean on Him. Believe me, I know it's hot. I understand."

"I don't think you do. You've always been so sure of your calling."

"I've been burned multiple times."

"You're not the one who saw it happen."

"I was there, Megan. Remember? I heard the shot. I came running."

"You weren't the one who shot and killed Guffey." Tears filled her eyes and spilled down her cheeks. "It seems all I can do is cry tonight."

"I wish I'd been there when he arrived. Then maybe you wouldn't be going through all this."

She closed her eyes. "And the blood...all the blood. Joni's lifeblood..."

He touched her wet cheek. "You saved the baby—you didn't kill the mother. She was already gone, and you know that."

"Cutting her like that." A sob escaped, and Megan raised her hands to her face as if she might be able to physically block the flow of emotion.

Gerard took her hands, and she let him. He drew her into his arms. She went. She pressed her forehead against his chest and wept.

"You not only stopped a psychopath on a murdering

spree, but you performed a postmortem C-section right there on the clinic floor and saved little Daria."

"It wasn't a C-section—it was an invasion. A slaughter."

"A rescue."

"And it shouldn't have had to happen. I knew how to shoot, I had my weapon, kept it close after Stud's death, but I still couldn't stop him." Megan looked up into Gerard's eyes. "I couldn't do anything to stop him, and I can never go back and redo it."

"Who knows how many other lives you saved when you took him down?" Gerard said softly. "Two days later Sean and I received a report that Bryant Guffey had killed at least sixteen people in other cities."

Megan caught her breath and withdrew. She reached into her shirt pocket and pulled out a tissue. She wiped her face, obviously struggling to put herself back together again.

"You'd have been next," Gerard said. "And then maybe Tess, or Sean or me."

"I've told myself that many times, but it's never enough."

"It's enough, Megan. More than enough. No police officer I know could have done what you did to save Daria."

"Except save her mom."

Gerard watched helplessly as the mask of cool control slipped back over Megan's face, belied only by her red eyes and nose. Once again she was withdrawing into herself. And yet she had relented and talked to her best friend about it. Granted, she'd most likely done so because she knew Lynley needed at least a few answers, but now that the subject had been broached, he had to believe Megan would feel some relief.

He reached up and dabbed at a stray tear on her cheek.

Unable to stop himself, he leaned down and placed a kiss on her forehead. "I guess we should take a look at this mansion." He pulled the lodge keys from his pocket. Kirstie had shown him which one opened the doors, and Megan held her light on the lock. The doors opened without a sound.

The place smelled faintly of a citrus grove. "Someone keeps this place up."

"Didn't Kirstie tell you?" Megan entered a magnificent great hall with gold-and-white-marbled floors and a carpeted staircase more than two stories high. "She's the caretaker. When it needs a deep cleaning she hires the help and oversees the work." She reached to the right and touched a circular light switch. "There's a grand piano, a stage and dance floor up the—" The lights came on and she cried out, grabbing Gerard's arm.

A man's body lay sprawled on the marble directly beneath the polished mahogany railing that edged the upper floor. Blood pooled beneath his head.

"Stay back." Gerard pressed her behind him and sprinted across the marble floor. He dropped to his knees beside the man and felt his carotid artery. The body was still warm, but he was dead.

"That's Barry Marshal," Megan said softly from the doorway.

FOURTEEN

On Monday evening Megan stepped from the crowded funeral home for some fresh air and looked at all the cars lined along the quiet street in Pierce City, a short drive from Jolly Mill. The lot behind the home was full. Practically every citizen of Jolly Mill and many Pierce City residents were here for the evening visitation and funeral being held for Barry Marshal.

After a day of storms and torrential rain, birds sang from the surrounding trees and the air smelled clean and pure. Megan wished her mind would feel so fresh after the storms in her life.

She wasn't surprised by the turnout despite Barry's questionable reputation. Folks in this part of the country attended funerals to support family, not necessarily to show respect for the dead. They reconnected to life, to each other, and if the deceased had been loved, then their friends focused on them and relived funny memories. Megan suspected that, for her community, attending a funeral was a way to come to terms with the limits placed on their own lives.

The door rattled behind her and Lynley stepped out, her heels echoing across the porch. Her dark eyes were rimmed with red, and her makeup had all been wiped off a couple of hours ago by the shoulders of friends and neighbors.

"You look awful," she said as she joined Megan at the edge of the porch.

"Thanks. You too."

"You heard his death was ruled an accident?" Lynley asked.

"I heard."

"What would my father have been doing in the lodge? Nora talked Mom into getting the locks changed after Dad moved out, so he didn't even have a workable set of keys, and there was no evidence of a break-in. Only Uncle Lawson, Mom and Nora had a master key. Have you heard the rumors flying around in there tonight?"

Megan had, but for the sake of Kirstie and Lynley she'd asked the people talking to keep their voices down. "A little."

"Now they're thinking Carmen or Nora might have had a private encounter with Dad at the lodge."

"Then they don't know either woman very well. Carmen doesn't even have a key."

"Nora does." Lynley crossed her arms and sighed as she leaned against the railing. "As if Nora would ever be stupid enough to have an affair with my father."

Megan studied her friend's face. "You've held up well." Despite the smudged and erased makeup.

"I've cried all evening and I can't understand why. It isn't as if my father ever loved me. We were never close."

"That in itself is something to cry about."

"Then you and I both have reason to cry. He didn't have much love for you either."

Megan recalled the very brief talk he'd had with her after she found him and Mom together. All he'd said was,

"Consider what you lose if you say a word. They'll hate you."

"I'm not crying," she told Lynley.

"No, but right now we've got all these shoulders offered to us, so we might as well take advantage of it. Emotionally healthy and all that."

"No more episodes with Kirstie?"

"None. Nora did exactly what she'd threatened to do—which you would know all about if you'd bothered to take a jaunt through the woods and visit us."

"What did Nora do?"

"She made Mom sleep with her these past two nights on the king bed in the guest room, complete with handcuffs she borrowed from Moritz."

Megan pressed her lips together for a second. "Oh, that is so wrong on so many levels."

"That's what Mom said, but Nora wouldn't relent. She said Kirstie would go swimming in the mill pond again over her dead and handcuffed body."

"You're serious?"

"No kidding. Any time one of them had to get up to go to the bathroom, the other had to go too."

Megan burst into laughter. "I didn't think Nora meant it when she made that threat."

"She's determined Mom won't go missing again. She also hired a housekeeper—a man named McDowell—to keep watch over Mom during the day. He's driving Mom crazy, but Nora's been teaching him to bake her cookie recipe, so she may offer him another job after his watch-dog role ends. It can't come too quickly for Mom. But there have been no more blackouts."

"It's early yet."

"Not really, Megan." Lynley hesitated, cleared her throat. "She had several episodes while I was with her these past few weeks. I just never let her leave the house, and it was our little secret."

"You didn't tell me?"

Lynley kicked her toe against the concrete step. "Didn't tell anyone. I kept picturing some men in white coats coming to take Mom away, and I couldn't let that happen, no matter what. It would have killed me."

Ouch. And Megan had been trying to make Lynley lock her mother away. "I'm sorry."

"I know."

"I'm glad we kept the clinic closed today. You needed to be with Kirstie."

"And you needed to be with Gerard?" Lynley spread her hands. "Just guessing, not interfering. I thought you wanted to avoid him."

"You know how much you love chocolate? Yet when you try to break the habit you crave it even more?"

Lynley grimaced. "I know that has to be difficult, especially since he's trying to set up shop here."

"You have no idea."

"You love him."

Megan nodded.

"Then what's the problem? He's obviously crazy about you. I mean, look at what the man's doing here. He's here because you are, plain and simple."

"First of all, I can't get Joni's death out of my mind, and with him here it's even worse. Second, sure he's here now, but what if he suddenly decided he needed to return to the mission in Texas?"

"I think he's made it clear he plans to settle here to be with you."

"But I need to love him enough to return with him to Corpus Christi if he goes. And I can't do that right now."

"Because you don't love him enough?"

"Because I'm terrified. Besides, my thoughts about God are not the best thoughts after what happened with Joni, and a shared faith is vital. I've seen that with your mom and dad. The spirit—whatever spirit it was—in Barry hated the Spirit in Kirstie."

"So which spirit do you choose? Barry's or Mom's? You've seen evidence of both. You've seen tons of evidence in Gerard. It kind of seeps out of him like sunlight through a clean window."

"I don't have what it takes to keep up with Gerard's God."

"Okay." Lynley placed a gentle hand on Megan's arm. "Take your time. Hey, seriously, you've missed so much action at the Thompson home the past three days."

"Fights between Nora and Kirstie?"

"Well, sure, there's that. You know Mom and Nora can't be in the same room for ten minutes without arguing. I think Nora loves the company, though, and she experimented with a new cookie recipe. I thought you'd at least stop by."

"You had a funeral to plan, and I didn't want to interfere."

"Stop that. You know you're family, even if I did behave like a shrew the other night."

"How have you felt over the weekend?"

Lynley's eyes narrowed as she studied Megan in silence for a moment. "Civil today. You and Nora both seem to think there's a leak or contaminant in the house that's affecting Mom, and maybe even me, though neither of you has come right out and said it."

Megan nodded.

"What kind of contaminant?"

"Wish I knew." Megan had picked up the mail for the clinic today. Kirstie's toxicology screen was negative, which wasn't surprising, but it was disappointing. Now they had to keep looking.

"You could have told me," Lynley said.

"It wasn't my call."

Lynley nodded. "Mom. There's nothing like a mother's loving protection to make a grown woman want to gnaw on bones."

The door opened and Gerard stepped out. "You ladies behaving?"

"What's it to you?" Megan stuck her tongue out at him. Their comfortable companionship had fallen back into place today as they'd worked together, side by side, silently searching for land and local history. No kisses, no romance, just friendship. He seemed to have known what she needed.

Gerard beckoned them. "Reverend Gripka's getting ready to start."

Lynley looked at Megan. "Do me a favor? Reverend Tom's probably going to have people stand up and say all kinds of nice things about Dad. If I start to interrupt or argue, pinch me?"

"If you'll do the same for me."

"Deal."

Kirstie sat between Lynley and Megan on the hard wooden pew in the front row of the funeral home. As she had expected, the minister breezed through the eulogy about Barry and segued into a short sermon about righteous living. She smiled. That was why she'd chosen him to conduct the service. No lies about the deceased. No ugly truths either. He left the attendees to form their own opinion about Barry amongst themselves.

The service concluded quickly, and she sat watching friends and neighbors as they filed past the casket and walked over to hug her and Lynley once more. She saw few tears, and she couldn't bring herself to shed more, though she'd managed to weep a time or two upon their arrival and when viewing the body, when she'd suddenly started to wonder what life would have been like if she'd married a man who had been steadfast as a husband and father. That was the saddest thing of all—Barry's choices.

During most of her adult years Kirstie had attended dozens of visitations and funerals, and she was typically replenished by them. Most of the funerals she'd attended had been for people who'd known for years that when they died they would be in Heaven. Barry had never cared. He had only maligned Kirstie for her faith.

She was hugging yet another neighbor when a familiar figure caught her attention from across the room. She felt herself tense. A few pieces of blackness fell away when she recognized Alec Thompson. Just Alec in a suit. But Alec seldom wore a suit, and the one he wore tonight was actually one his father had once worn in his sales job. How strange that it looked fashionable on Alec's broad shoulders. Fashion always went in cycles.

How much the son looked like the father, Eaton, except for the dark, exotic eyes of his mother.

She tapped Megan on the shoulder. "Honey, how old was Alec when his father left on that hunting trip and never returned?"

Megan looked up from the memorial card she was reading and glanced toward Alec. "We were seventeen. We'd been dating a few months."

Kirstie hugged Barry's aunt Sally and gently agreed that this was a loss for the community. Obviously, Barry hadn't been able to face his own blood kin with the truth about abandoning his wife. It was a mercy, in some ways, that Barry's parents had already passed on.

When Sally walked unsteadily down the aisle, Kirstie turned back to Megan. "How did Alec react to his father's abandonment?"

"Upset." Megan frowned. "He kept waiting for his dad to return, and he and Nora actually asked rangers to search Eaton's favorite camping spot in Mark Twain National Forest. They found the truck but not Eaton. Because the truck was parked in a campground in Missouri, all anyone could figure was there'd been an accidental shooting and he was too deep in the brush to be found. Believe it or not, I think Alec might have been a little relieved too. Life at home wasn't smooth for him."

"Did his father hit him?"

"No, never. You know Nora would never let anyone lay a hand on Alec. I think if she could've gone to Afghanistan with him, she'd have done it. But if you're worried about how Lynley's going to handle Barry's passing, she'll handle this okay. She's a lot older than Alec was."

Kirstie gave a brief shake of her head. "Nora never talked much about her life with Eaton, but I knew he wasn't a kind person. I'm not sure why, but Eaton keeps coming to my mind. Doesn't Alec look a lot like his father?"

Megan wrinkled her nose and glanced down the line of well-wishers. "I don't remember much about him except his breath. Alec doesn't drink much. I think he's more like Nora."

More pieces of Kirstie's blacked-out memories fell into place, both recent and past. The circle took shape again—and it was the size of a man's ring. It had a topaz in the center of it, with sharp edges that could cut skin.

Kirstie nudged Megan's shoulder again. "Remember the ring Eaton always wore? He never took it off. It was shaped like a lion's head with a topaz. He used to hit

Barry in the face the night Barry asked him to leave the restaurant for disorderly conduct."

"I remember the scar he left." Megan straightened and looked around the room. "Lawson was putting in that new addition, remember? He was getting ready to pour a foundation for a huge sunroom between the lodge ballroom and restaurant and the suites. Didn't Barry tell everyone he'd fallen in the site where the construction workers were digging the foundation?"

"He was embarrassed to have anyone know Eaton gave him that gash."

"What about the ring, Kirstie? Is that the one you keep seeing in your blackouts?"

"It could be. Things seem to be falling back into place a little at a time."

"Lynley said you're doing better."

Kirstie nodded. But why was she so focused on Eaton's ring?

Alec drew closer in the line—moving slowly, of course, because everyone knew the minister, everyone knew each other, and half the people didn't even seem to consider that they were in any kind of line, they were just there to hang out and talk.

Kirstie glanced at Alec's hands. No rings of any kind. Unlike his father, Alec was not into ostentation. Also unlike his father, Alec was not cruel. Kirstie remembered that on her second date with Eaton, he picked her up with alcohol on his breath and got belligerent when she called him on it.

She'd warned Nora about him, but Nora had always been tougher than Kirstie—not as sweet. Definitely not a people-pleaser. For years Kirstie lived in admiration of Nora, that she could marry a man as hard to handle as Eaton, raise a sweet son, build an empire without Eaton's inebriated help. Also, to Kirstie's shame, she'd been relieved for her friend when Eaton took off on one of his weeklong hunting trips and simply didn't return.

Still, as Kirstie hugged Alec and gave him a quick kiss on the cheek, she wondered. Alec had always had his father's build and strength. Perhaps she should have paid more attention to Nora, her son and their needs when their husband and father disappeared, but Nora appeared to be handling everything fine, as she always did, and at that time there were other heartbreaks on which to focus.

About the time Eaton took off, Uncle Lawson was diagnosed with lung cancer. Unable to find anyone else to run the whole operation and too ill to run it himself, Lawson was forced to shut down the resort. He didn't need the income. He never opened the resort again.

Today before the funeral Kirstie had finally worked up the nerve to call Lawson and break the news to him about Barry.

"Sorry to hear about that, sugar," he'd said in his deep voice. "I have to say the timing is interesting. I was just getting ready to cut his name from the will, and now I won't have to."

That had surprised her. "But why? You always loved Barry."

"I have no time for a man who doesn't have enough love and loyalty to see his wife through the hardships of life."

"You knew he left?"

"You have friends who aren't afraid to hurt my feelings, Kirstie. I just wish you'd been willing to stick up for yourself. You know, now that I think about it, I'm still taking any of his accidental offspring out of the will, just in case."

Since he'd brought up the subject, Kirstie had decided to mention something that had been on her mind a lot these past few days. "Uncle Lawson, speaking of the will. You know I'm not going to have the knowledge or ability to run the resort."

"Don't worry. I knew what you had in mind when you brought Vance here the other day."

Tears had smarted Kirstie's eyes. She would miss Lawson so much. "Is that going to affect your will?"

"If he follows through with his plans, the place is his. I've checked the whole family out and I can't think of a better group of people to do what they're doing."

"Neither can I."

"It'll mean less for you and Eugene."

"You think either of us cares about the money, Uncle Lawson? You've been the treasure in our lives."

There was a long silence, and Kirstie had heard the flow of oxygen. "I love you too, baby. Come and see me in a few days. Bring Vance back with you if you can. We need to get this all hashed out while I can still think straight."

"We'll be there," she had assured him.

The funeral music fell silent, and Megan placed an arm around Kirstie's shoulders, drawing her from her melancholy. "Hey, don't tell me you're blacking out again. What's on your mind? Everyone's waiting for us to follow the casket out. We're going to the cemetery."

Kirstie glanced at Nora standing beside Carmen and their friends at the back of the chapel. So many other friends had stood beside her through this awful time. She prayed a silent blessing for them as she walked down the aisle beside Lynley, followed by Megan. She had been given a wonderful gift in her friendships.

After the interment Megan drove home alone, despite multiple invitations to join the family at Nora's. Gerard would be there. She needed time to slow down and think, and there'd been so little of it today. When she was with Gerard, even working silently by his side, she was so focused on him she couldn't focus on anything else. The struggle wore her out.

Actually, what wore her out was trying not to think about being without him—especially if he settled here, as it appeared he was determined to do.

She stepped into the empty cottage, dropped her dressy carryall beside the door and locked up behind her. She had a drink of water and eyed the bed, tempted to lie down and sleep without her usual nightly ritual of changing into her pajamas and brushing her teeth…she was so tired.

And yet, tired as she was, she needed to make one call before she went to sleep. She'd waited on purpose until after the funeral. She dug her cell phone from the bag and pressed her mother's number. And braced herself. It had been at least six weeks since she'd spoken to any family members. They didn't know what was happening in her life right now, not even her brother because he was horrible at keeping secrets.

The evening sky still held a touch of light from the long-set sun, reminding Megan that the storm had passed completely and summer was on its way. They would still be in for a few more storms—at least, she hoped so. They needed more water than they'd received today.

Her mother answered on the third ring.

"Megan? Is this really you?" Mom's typical sarcasm. "Are you dying or something?"

Megan gave a long-suffering sigh. "Hi, Mom. I'm not dying."

"What are you doing up so late? It's nearly nine."

Another snide remark about Megan's typical early bedtime. She grimaced. "I didn't know if anyone from Jolly Mill had called you."

"Only three of my old high school buddies. They'd thought for sure you'd have let us know you'd moved back to Jolly Mill to take a job at the clinic. Not something I would expect to hear from my own daughter, of course, but other people are innocent to our ways. Why'd you leave the job you had, and who are you staying with?"

Megan rolled her eyes, ignoring the first question. "I'm in the Thompson cottage. Uh, listen, I just returned home from a funeral and thought you might want to be warned that we found Barry Marshal dead at the Barnes Lodge and Resort on Friday."

Silence. What, no snide remarks about that?

"Anyway," Megan said, "I didn't want you to hear about it later and be taken off guard."

"And just how did you think it would take me off guard?"

"I didn't know." It wasn't as if they really knew each other. "Look, it's been a long evening and I'm tired. I just wanted to give you the heads-up."

"Thank you for the warning, but Megan, you're way off base if you think I'm going to be upset."

Megan's turn for silence. Was that actually a gentle note in her mother's voice?

"You there, Megan? I'm serious. Barry Marshal has been a bad memory since the first moment I let him touch me."

Megan held the phone from her ear. She didn't really want to hear that.

"He was never a friend of mine," Mom was saying when Megan put the phone back to her ear. "He was the biggest mistake I ever made, especially when you walked in the door and found us. I've never been more sorry for anything in my life."

Megan's throat was so dry she could barely swallow. "Wow. And you couldn't have told me that sooner?"

"Would you have listened?"

"Eventually. Did you ever tell Dad?"

"No, did you?"

"No."

"I did tell Kirstie what kind of husband she had," Mom said. "And I got myself tested for any kind of disease before I let your father...well...you know."

Megan jerked the phone away again. Too much information.

"Anyway," her mother continued, "your father's retiring in six weeks, and he's promised me we're going to travel together from now on. You know, if you got over here more often you'd be able to see how things have changed."

Megan sank onto the bed. "Kirstie really knows?"

"She always has, Megan. She even promised me she would get tested."

The silence lengthened on the line until Megan wondered if they'd lost the connection. All these years Kirstie knew, and she'd never said a word. Megan felt as if the sands in her hourglass had broken through their barrier and were spilling out all over the place. Had she held on to this anger with her mother over something they could have discussed and settled years ago?

"Wow."

Her mother chuckled. "Yeah, I know. We'll talk about this some more, I hope, but you need to know that I've always been crazy about Dad. That thing with Barry wasn't love. It wasn't even—"

"Yeah, I get it. Don't use the words, okay? Kids don't want to hear these things about their parents."

Another chuckle. What on earth was going on with Mom?

"Anyway, I hated the travel, all the time alone, raising my kids without the daily input from their father, and I realized, almost too late, that my anger was going to destroy my marriage. And I loved your father too much for that to happen."

Megan's mind flashed to Gerard. "Thanks for that, Mom."

"Why don't you drive to Cape Girardeau soon? If I recall correctly, there's no room for us to stay in that cottage of Nora's."

"I might do that."

"And now it's really past your bedtime," Mom said. "I appreciate your call, though, Megan."

"Okay. Well, then, I'll talk to you…soon."

"It's always good to hear from you, Megan. If you called more often, maybe I wouldn't be caught off guard."

"I guess not. Bye."

She punched the disconnect button and then hit Gerard's speed dial before she could react to the shock of her call. "Hi," she told his voice mail. "Even though the tox screen didn't show anything, I still believe there's a toxin in that house. I don't think it's coincidence Kirstie is doing better at Nora's. We need to get a specialist to check the vents, and you should probably find another place to stay. I just happened to remember that because it's been cold at night lately, Kirstie would have had the heat on, and several toxins become more potent with heat, including mercury. Barry would have had access to mercury several years ago."

She disconnected, switched off the phone, slumped over into bed and closed her eyes. Maybe she could sleep without a pill tonight.

FIFTEEN

Gerard found the mercury at seven o'clock on Tuesday morning when he pulled the vent screens from the master suite of Kirstie's house. A test with a local metallurgist confirmed his suspicion.

The whole town of Jolly Mill knew about the mercury by the end of the day when a hazmat team from Springfield combed through the building and checked other houses around it. Only Kirstie's had been affected. All sheet metal had to be replaced, which Monett Sheet Metal promised to do.

Gerard was reeling when he heard the news. People responded quickly around here, especially when it meant helping others.

Suspicion rested on Barry for the mercury, of course. His father had been a local dentist for many years, and Barry would have had access to the mercury used at the time as an ingredient to fill teeth. When vaporized, that same ingredient had the power to kill.

Gerard could not have been more impressed by the quick responses. He knew business was slow in this area and people were hungry for income, which just reinforced his determination to give them what they wanted when

Kirstie asked him to have the whole house checked, re-wired and cleaned of any possible toxin.

Late Wednesday morning Gerard found the perfect place for Vance Manufacturing, where a garment factory had once operated at the edge of town. A fire had taken out the factory, and the owners had moved to Monett, de-capitating the tax income for Jolly Mill. The place was inside city limits with access to city utilities, and the new Vance manufacturing plant would more than replace the loss for Jolly Mill. It was also within walking distance of the lodge and resort.

Thirty minutes after making an inquiry on the sale of the place, Gerard's cell rang at Nora's place, where he had moved with Kirstie and Lynley. He was told the property had been rezoned for residential last Friday.

Last Friday. Soon after he spoke with Alec Thompson about his project.

Gerard paced across the bedroom—Nora had informed him this was Alec's old bedroom. That just irritated him further. He wanted to throw something. The target would likely be Alec Thompson. Why was the man impeding progress for the town and help for people who so desper-ately needed it?

Gerard called the clinic and told Megan what his morn-ing had been like. It felt good to hear her compassionate voice on the other end of the line.

"Something's up, Gerard," Megan said. In the back-ground phones rang and people chattered, and Gerard knew he'd caught her at a busy time.

"Like what?"

"I've never known Alec to be so bullheaded. He's always been fair in business dealings. So has Nora. There's got to be some kind of catch here."

"I'd like to know what. Want to meet me for lunch?"

"That's in thirty minutes, you know."

"I can get a picnic basket together. Nora's housekeeper is at loose ends now that Kirstie's doing so much better, and though Nora has a lot of spare room, I'm getting really claustrophobic. Especially in Alec's old room. Maybe we can brainstorm some answers."

"Sounds good. Meanwhile I'll pick Carmen's brain and see what patients are saying about it when they come in. I know Carmen's still gung ho for your plan."

"And you?" As soon as he asked the question, he wasn't sure he was ready for the answer. "How do you feel about it? I got the impression you were uncomfortable bringing possibly dangerous people to a peaceful town."

"I've seen some close brushes with death lately, and not all of them came from Corpus Christi. I'm open to suggestions."

He grinned. "Well, that's not as great as gung ho, but it'll have to do."

"What I'm saying is there are no guarantees in life. Right?"

"Right."

"But we can't give up on life's script just because we didn't get it in writing."

"Now you sound like Tess." And that was encouraging.

"Or Lynley or Nora or Kirstie, take your pick."

He chuckled. He was going to like living here. He only wanted to make sure Megan stayed where she was. "I've called the newspaper and asked for citizens to show up at the specially called zoning committee meeting Thursday night. They need to know what the committee is doing and what they could lose if they allow this to happen. I do know how to play the political game."

"Yep. You can do that. Just don't ram it down their

throats or they'll resent it. I still think there must be some
kind of reason Alec doesn't want the plant here."

"It could have something to do with why he attempted
to purchase a piece of Lawson's property six years ago. It
wasn't for sale. I wonder if he still has his heart set on it.
That could be why he doesn't want our homeless here."

"What part of the resort did he want to purchase?"

"He wanted the lodge, ballroom and restaurant portion
of the resort and the unfinished sunroom."

"But why fight you? It's going to be yours. Lawson already put it in writing."

Gerard loved the sound of encouragement in her voice.
"We'll have to wait and see. Sandwich or fried chicken for
lunch?"

"Whatever you bring is fine."

When Gerard picked up Megan at noon, she could smell
a spicy tang of garlic and glanced at the genuine picnic
hamper in the backseat. "Pizza?"

"In sandwich form." He backed out of the parking spot.
"By morning, anyone who receives a paper will know
about the meeting, and if they read the letters to the editor
they'll know how I feel about it. I'm not sure if that'll be
enough, but I hope the town hall won't be able to hold the
crowd."

"Fighting form, I see." She reached into the backseat
and lifted one side of the hamper. "Mind if I eat? I'm
starved. No breakfast. I slept late."

"Have at it. Did Carmen have any information?"

Megan pulled out half a pepperoni and cheese on a
sourdough bun. "Strangely, no. Carmen was quiet for
once." She took a huge bite and savored the blend of tastes.
Sourdough was her favorite bread in the world. "Who
made this?" she asked with a half-full mouth.

"I did. Housekeeper was out. Is that strange?"

"What?"

"Carmen being quiet?"

Megan chewed and swallowed as he drove through town and turned right. "You'd better believe it. Carmen has an opinion about everything, and she's not afraid to share it."

"So you think she knows something we don't?"

Megan took another bite and shrugged. She'd never known Carmen to be quiet about anything, so this was new to her.

By the time Gerard parked the car, Megan had finished her half sandwich and was rummaging through the hamper for more food. Banana, apples...cookies! "What are these?"

"Oatmeal, coconut, pecan and dark chocolate. Nora made them last night. That woman cooks when she's stressed, and she's pretty much stressed all the time."

"I could've told you that." Megan bit into the dream cookie. Okay, this was her new favorite. "Let her stay stressed. It's good for the whole community."

"Maybe I'll take a batch of Nora's cookies to the meeting tomorrow night."

"Good idea. Serve them with coffee so everyone will stay up all night thinking about what you had to say."

Gerard accepted the sandwich Megan handed him. "I believe I can convince most folks of the benefits my proposal can offer the town."

"I know you can." Megan opened the door and stepped out. The grass was calf-deep and she could possibly step on a snake, but it had stormed again last night and the scent of the air was irresistible.

"So, Gerard, are you sure this is where God wants you?" She closed the door and took another bite of her cookie while Gerard joined her. A path led through an open gate to a waterfall in a hillside that faced south to a field, and they strolled toward the splashing water.

"I have no doubt. Kirstie told me that Lawson Barnes wants his property to go to the rehab center. I think I have my answer, don't you?"

"Even if you have to purchase outside the city limits, dig a well and do the infrastructure? It'll cost a lot more."

"I don't think we'll have to build outside the city limits. Once people know how much revenue this could bring to Jolly Mill, I feel sure a vote will swing our way."

Megan sank onto a boulder beside the splashing waterfall. "I don't know how you keep going," she said quietly. "You've had so many setbacks, seen so much ugliness. You have seen people at their worst and yet you keep going, helping, giving."

"How many times have I told you I don't do it myself?"

"I know, God does it through you, but you're still in the midst of it, and I don't see you getting a break."

"You don't think the Barnes property is a break? Megan, God's in control of everything, every struggle."

"Then why does it seem that every time you're right in the middle of doing something good, you get hit hardest with trials and pain? Why was it your fiancé left you when she found out you were devoting Vance money to the mission?" Megan wanted to slap her own mouth for letting those words fall out of it like that.

Gerard didn't hesitate. "She had the free will to make that decision."

"But you were sure enough she was God's choice for you that you were willing to make that kind of commitment to her, yet you were obviously wrong. How do you know this rehab project is right? How can you know you're doing God's will? If you'd pursued a different profession, would you be happily married now?"

"I can't think that way." Gerard sat down beside her and took the final bite of his sandwich. He sat staring into the rush of water as if mesmerized, then he glanced at the huge cookie Megan held in her hand. "You going to eat that whole thing and continue to fit into your scrubs?"

Megan scowled at him and took another bite. "There are more back in the hamper. I saw them. If you'd wanted one you could have brought it with you."

He chuckled. "Ann left me because she discovered I was planning to devote all my excess financial resources to the mission. Typically, like any man, I thought she was in love with me when she was actually in love with my family money. We all have blind places. That just means we have to draw closer to God and pray for wisdom. That's a prayer He's promised to answer."

"I used to pray." Megan broke off a piece of cookie and handed it to Gerard. "As a child, I knew how. My parents sent me to Sunday school."

"But you forgot how to pray?"

"I just didn't see the point in it. Nothing ever changed."

"How do you know?"

"My mother had the affair."

"And yet your parents are still married. People make mistakes, Megan. Bad ones. I'm sure that right now, Ann is deeply disappointed that she gave up the chance to marry a man like me."

Megan chuckled as she was expected to, then took a bite of the cookie and watched the water, thinking of her family. "Dad worked so hard all his life that he didn't spend enough time with Mom. She took it out on me. I asked Dad to make her stop, but he never could. There wasn't enough of him to go around. Maybe, like Dad, God's too busy to spend time on my silly requests."

"This world isn't our permanent home, Megan. We're going to struggle here. It's written in the Bible. You've been through some storms. Awful ones."

"Storms I can't deal with."

"You haven't had the time to deal with this last one. I hope you know I've been praying for God to give you peace, but despite all, I think your presence here may be a calling from God."

Megan frowned up at him. "Here? In Jolly Mill? I haven't heard any call."

"You came here, didn't you? God is a great casting director." Gerard reached toward her, and for a moment she thought he was after the rest of her cookie. She held it away from him.

He touched her face, then leaned forward and kissed her forehead. "It's been stormy lately—not just the weather, but the situation. But Christ knows how to calm the storms in our lives. We find Him in our hardest times, our deepest valleys, and we don't always have to use words to pray. There are times when we can't come up with the words. He has to do it for us."

Any other time she would have argued, but for some reason his words resonated. She thought about her old Sunday school teacher, Martha Irene, and her prayer pillows, and the pillow that seemed to anchor her to reality the night Gerard came to the cottage.

"You think Kirstie and Lynley would have moved in with Nora if I hadn't convinced them?" she asked.

"Maybe not. We may not know the answer to that in this lifetime."

Megan gave him the last of her cookie. Could God really be in this? And if so, why use her?

"I would never marry a man for his money," she said.

"I know."

"I had begun to think maybe you and I...you know... might be right for each other," she said. "But I've realized that I'm not right for you."

"I thought perhaps you'd decided I wasn't right for you."

"No. There's a big difference. You need a woman who's strong and filled with love for God and ready to plunge right into your mission."

"Why?"

"Well, because that's what you need. Someone to work beside you."

"Are you saying I can't do the job I've been doing all these years by myself?"

Megan shook her head. "I practically grew up in church, you know. My parents didn't attend much, but I was there all the time, especially when I stayed with the Marshals because Kirstie was always active in her church, and I spent a lot of weekends with them. After catching my mother with Barry, and after I saw all Kirstie and Lynley went through because of Barry's behavior, I pretty much gave up on waiting for God to come along and make things right again."

"What do you feel God should have done, when it was human choice that caused the suffering in the first place?"

Megan shrugged. "All I know is that one day I flat-out told God I didn't want to be a pawn in His game of chess any longer. I didn't see how living by His rules made things any easier than living without them. In fact, I saw more Christians suffer than unbelievers."

"You can't see into the human heart, though, Megan. And you can't see past this life. If you could see things from God's point of view—"

"Which I can't—"

"—then you'd see a whole different picture."

"But there's never a break for you, Gerard. I mean, you take hit after hit and you keep on going, and I can't see how you do it. You talk about storms. I know hurricanes are long and destructive, but even with them there's always an eye to the storm. You never get that eye."

"Oh, yes I do. The storm is always there, but since you arrived at the mission, you've been the eye to my storm. When I see families find a home, that's an eye to my storm. We help people who will never stand on their own two feet and take care of themselves, but we also see happy endings. Those are great breaks. But Megan, since you came to us, I've always believed you were going to be the relief I needed. I don't need someone to work beside me, but I would like someone there when I get home at night."

Megan caught her breath. He'd never spoken so forthrightly before. "And I left."

"The way I saw it, you left the pain of the mission, and you were called here for a reason. I never considered that you left me personally."

"But I don't have the strength it takes to live the kind of life you live."

"I didn't ask you to. All I ask is that you follow God's calling for you, not His calling for me. I saw something in you there that seemed to grow the longer you were at the mission, and it was for patients. You just got caught in a terror that wasn't of your making. You're wounded now, but you learn and grow from tragedies such as this so that maybe you'll be able to recognize it when it happens again."

"It's not going to happen to me."

"You can't hide from life, and you can't continue to blame yourself for someone else's evil."

His chin was so firm, his blue eyes so confident. He had a faith she'd never be able to comprehend. There was no mistaking the strength in his expression.

"You can't predict the future, Megan." His voice washed her with tenderness. "You had no way of knowing what that crazed man would do."

"But I should have realized he was drugged. I should have known there was a possibility he would try something." She should have made Joni leave the exam room when the killer first stepped through the door.

The nightmare was suddenly surrounding her again. She couldn't do this. "I had a weapon I could have used in time to protect her and her unborn baby." No matter how often she'd tried, she could not forget watching the life leave Joni's eyes.

"Don't take this burden alone, Megan."

"I could never go back to Corpus Christi," she said. "Which is why I'm not right for you. God may call you back there someday, and I wouldn't be able to go." She felt the quiver in her voice.

"I'm not leaving Jolly Mill. You should know me well enough by now to realize I'm not going to end something I've started if it's a good idea, and following you here was a good idea." He motioned toward the field in front of them. "See this? As of yesterday, I own it."

She gazed out across the field, the creek running through the middle, the trees around a pond. "You're putting the manufacturing plant here?"

"No, I hope to build a home here. I want to make this my home. You wouldn't have to go back to Corpus Christi. I would never make you do that."

She stood up and brushed the crumbs from her scrubs. "You don't understand, Gerard. If I'm not willing to follow you anywhere, I'm not right for you. That's all there is to it." She walked slowly back to the car as her heart felt as if it would swell to bursting despite her brave words to him. To be loved like this by a man like this? A man she loved? She wanted to turn and run back to him and jump into his arms and never let go.

The pain she felt as she continued to walk away was as if she was being ripped in half. She may not love him enough to follow him back to Texas, but she loved him enough to free him to find someone who did.

SIXTEEN

On Thursday night, while Gerard went armed with Nora's cookies and gourmet coffee to the town hall meeting, Megan answered a call from Kirstie to meet with her at the lodge. The timing was strange, but Kirstie's voice also sounded strange. Fearing another blackout, Megan drove the long way around in case she needed to drive Kirstie back down the hill.

She entered the same door she and Gerard had entered last Friday night. This time the lights were all on, the chandeliers gleaming on the burnished tables and woodwork, reflecting from the leaded glass windows. The marble floor had been cleaned of blood, but if Megan blinked she could see the stain of it surrounding Barry's head.

"Up here," Kirstie called from the top of the stairs. "I've been studying the banister."

Kirstie took the carpeted stairway to join her friend. "Are you okay?"

"Not really." Kirstie stepped over to the railing above the place on the floor where Megan and Gerard had found Barry. "This banister? Sheriff Moritz should have noticed that it's not the least bit loose. And though Barry was a tall man, unless he intentionally climbed over this railing and jumped, he couldn't have accidentally fallen."

Megan grasped the banister and shook it for Kirstie's benefit, but she'd gone over this whole thing in her mind since finding him. "What if he did jump?"

"Barry? I don't think so. A man who's trying to poison his wife—and possibly his daughter—for a large sum of money is not going to commit suicide."

"Then you believe someone could have murdered him?"

Kirstie gazed down at the marble floor, and her face softened. "No. I can't think that either. Uncle Lawson wouldn't have done it even if he'd had the strength. And Gerard had a set of my keys, but he wouldn't have had a reason to kill a complete stranger."

"The only other person with a set—"

"Is Nora." Kirstie's facial features twisted with sorrow and pain. "I can't believe it of her. Not Nora. She's no killer."

"Of course not."

"But I found Eaton's ring the other day in Nora's attic, and I recalled seeing it before. Remember two years ago when Nora broke her leg? I moved in with her for a while to take care of her until she could get around on her own. I was cleaning in her bedroom when I accidentally knocked over a jewelry case, and the ring fell out."

"He probably didn't wear his ring when he went hunting."

"He never took it off. He told me that when we went out on our first date. It was a gift from his father, and since his father's death he never removed that ring. Did you know Eaton was a mean drunk?"

"I knew about his reputation."

The sound of footsteps reached them from below. "I thought I saw lights," Nora Thompson called up to them.

"And so I took a stroll." She started up the stairs, and when her gaze caught her best friend's she didn't look away. "I stepped inside and looked around, checked out the kitchen. You know I used to play chef here part-time?"

"I remember," Kirstie said softly.

"I heard voices and came out to chat." She reached the top of the stairs and turned to look down them. "Sound carries well in this huge area."

"I know. Nora, I'm—"

"I had Alec attempt to purchase this building and the new area Lawson had in his plans. I told Alec the property values were only going up on this side of the creek, and we should invest while we had a chance. I wanted him to get into the game. Unfortunately, Alec's never enjoyed the investment game the way I have."

"Nora—"

"Lawson wasn't interested in selling." Nora stepped over to the piano and ran her fingers along the polished rim. "Our sins find us out, even when they aren't really sins."

"What happened?" Megan asked.

"Honey, are you sure you can't convince that man of yours to build elsewhere?"

"I thought you wanted the rehab center here."

"Not right here, Megan."

"Why?"

"Kirstie, you were right about Eaton. I wished so many times that I'd listened to you, but you know I'm not the best at paying attention. He was a bully. He came home drunk one night and pushed a little harder than ever before, hit me once too often. I honestly didn't mean to kill him, but the bottle didn't break. I broke his skull."

Kirstie gasped. "Oh, Nora."

"I'd have called the sheriff if it had been Moritz, but it

wasn't. It was Sandoll, and he and Eaton were the best of buddies. I could have pled self-defense, but no one knew Eaton was doing what he was to me at home."

"Alec?" Megan asked.

Nora shook her head. "Eaton was on his best behavior when his son was home. He was good about hitting me where it didn't show." She sat down on the piano bench and leaned forward. "I knew what Barry was doing, Kirstie. I went to him and threatened to tell you about his philandering ways if he didn't help me make Eaton disappear. I was that desperate." She looked up at Kirstie with tears in her eyes. "I'm sorry."

"What did he do with Eaton's body?" Kirstie asked.

Nora reached into the pocket of her slacks and pulled out a lethal-looking .380 semi-automatic.

People were chowing down on Nora's cookies during a break. Gerard couldn't have asked for a better crowd. He shot a glance toward Alec across the table, and Alec caught his eye for just a moment. They nodded to each other.

"Nora Thompson is going to owe us a bundle for this" came a quiet voice from behind the coffee urn. "Vance is making more and more sense."

Gerard looked up to see surprise register on Alec's face.

"She'll make it up to us," came another voice. "She always does. Just vote and keep your mouth shut."

The voices grew softer as the men walked away.

Gerard met Alec's gaze again. "I thought your mother was in favor of the rehab center."

"So did I."

"Then doesn't she realize the manufacturing plant needs the rehab center in order to work?"

Alec shrugged. "Maybe if you sold the Barnes place

to her at a decent price, she'll see to it you get the zoning you want in a different place."

"I'm not denying a man his dying wish. If she has the money, she can build her own resort."

"You don't know my mom very well."

Gerard had come to know that Nora Thompson usually got what she wanted. So what was it she wanted?

Something didn't feel right. Badly as Gerard wanted to stay and fight this battle, he couldn't get Megan's latest message from his mind. She was meeting with Kirstie at the lodge right now. The lodge Nora wanted badly enough to undermine his plans with the town.

He grabbed his notes and left.

Kirstie stared at the gun in Nora's hand. "Honey, what on earth are you doing with that thing?"

Nora pushed the bench backward and stood up. "I'd have thought you would recognize this. It was Barry's."

"What?"

"After Barry took care of Eaton's body so easily, I knew what he was capable of. So when word spread that Lawson was given such a short time to live, I wondered if Barry might pull something. And he did. Soon after, you started having your blackouts. I called him and had him meet me here one day, and I told him I knew what he was up to and that if anything happened to you I was going to tell the police about Eaton and have Barry investigated. That was when I told him he had to move out."

"You're the one who did that?"

"I thought he was putting something in your food, dropping something in your drinks, and if he left, it would stop. But it didn't stop. It kept getting worse. Last Friday I called another meeting." She held up the gun. "He brought this with him and pulled it on me." She let the gun dangle between her fingers and held it out to Kirstie. "The idiot must have forgotten I've been practicing martial arts for years."

"Self-defense." Kirstie took the weapon. "Again."

"Kirstie, you're my best friend. I've done all I could to protect myself, but Barry told me a few years ago he'd buried Eaton's body here on the grounds. They were pouring concrete for the sunroom and they didn't complete the job because Lawson got sick. My husband's body is buried beneath a very thin layer of concrete, so the moment someone starts to excavate, the body will be found, and I'll be arrested."

"Barry thought you would hide his dirty little secrets because he helped you hide your accident?" Kirstie shook her head. "He didn't know you at all. Honey, Alec's a grown man now. You don't have to protect him, and this town loves you. Come clean with Moritz. Clear the air."

"I'm guilty of obstructing justice, and I could be found guilty of two murders."

"Have a little faith, Nora. People in this town know you, and we all know you're not a killer. Let it go. Get out from under all this."

"And the first thing you can do," came Gerard Vance's voice from below, "is call off your committee and make the right zone change."

At the sound of Gerard's voice, Megan realized she hadn't been running from Corpus Christi at all. The truth fell over her as if the sun had burst forth over the room. What had frightened her so badly was the thought that someday Gerard could be killed.

Losing Joni had not only undermined her confidence in herself, but the loss broke her heart. Period. She was afraid to love Gerard and lose him.

Megan took the gun from Kirstie, slid back the clip to check it for ammo and found it empty. She slid the pistol into her pocket and turned to greet Gerard.

Kirstie put her arm around Nora and led her down the stairs. "We need to find you a good attorney."

"I know two of them. Maybe more would be better."

"Why don't you go ahead and call Moritz, get the jump on everything, turn yourself in?"

"Attorneys first, Kirs. You know I like to do things a certain way."

"You know I love my tigress of a best friend."

"Well, I guess you can be pretty certain that I love you too."

SEVENTEEN

Megan ached from her toes to her fingertips by the time she reached Corpus Christi the first day of June. How had she forgotten the heat in such a short time? She'd become accustomed to the hot and humid air of Jolly Mill and forgotten it could be even hotter elsewhere.

She took the last exit before the bridge and made her way through traffic. He would be at the mission. Gerard couldn't go to Corpus Christi without spending time at the mission, even if Tess and Sean had taken over management. Gerard was supposed to be moving his household furniture to storage so Tess and Sean could move in.

The house Gerard was having built wouldn't be complete for another month, so meanwhile he was back in Kirstie's upstairs suite, overseeing the arrival of household staff at the new Vance Rehab Facility.

Megan thought about calling Tess one more time to make sure he was there, but if Gerard was anywhere near the phone it might ruin the surprise.

After two more telephone calls to her parents, Megan had ironed out most of her problems with Mom. Interesting how much alike they were. And frightening. But Mom had changed over the years, and Megan hadn't noticed.

It was time. Things did change. People changed. Even Megan.

Nora, of course, had not only a group of attorneys on her case, but she hadn't spent a single night in jail. Alec had at first been devastated to discover his mother's dark secrets, but despite his father's attempts to cover up his cruelty, Alec had suspected for many years. He too was on better terms with his mother these days. Maybe he and Megan had both matured a little these past few weeks.

Vance Manufacturing was halfway completed, with Hans overseeing the work and living at the rehab center. He never lacked for food or female attention, and though Megan had made several attempts to introduce him to her best friend, Lynley was back in her own home in Columbia, studying for her doctorate in nursing.

Megan pulled into the parking lot behind the mission and found a spot. Granted, her heart rate was slightly elevated, but she couldn't tell for sure if that was from bad memories or the realization that she'd driven all the way down here to propose. What if he turned her down?

Old friends and residents rushed to greet her as soon as she stepped through the back door. She hugged several necks as she made her way toward the door to admin. Before she reached it, though, she glanced through the window to see a familiar head of blond hair bent over the physician's desk.

He looked up as if he sensed her arrival. He met her before she could take three steps into the clinic. "Megan?"

She took a breath. "I missed you."

He grinned. "I'm flying back tomorrow."

"Want to ride back with me? Save money?"

He put an arm around her and turned to look at the clinic. "We've put walls up. Seven exam rooms. Two full-time nurses, a nurse practitioner and a physician."

"I know. I was the one who told you to hire them and build the walls."

"Wanted to check me out and make sure I wasn't lying to you?"

She took his hand and tugged him back out the door. They'd had some good talks out walking along the streets that surrounded the mission. Granted, it wasn't the best part of town, but it was where they found the neediest people.

"I hate to admit it," she said, "but you were right. I was running from something I'll never be able to avoid, not even in Jolly Mill."

"You mean life?" He released her hand and put his arm around her again.

"I went out to your property the other day and prayed for you to have a good life, for some of your dreams to come true. But just standing on that land and praying for you didn't cut it for me." She recalled the sudden burst of joy she'd felt that day.

"At least you're back on speaking terms with God."

"I'm beginning to see His viewpoint more often. I'm realizing I never lost faith in Him, I was just angry. You don't get angry with someone if you don't believe in them."

"I knew that. So Megan, tell me why you're here. You said you'd never come back."

"I was wrong. I wanted to prove it."

"Well, I hope you're not here for a job, because it's filled."

"Nope." She grinned. "Got one."

"It's going to get busier pretty quickly too. You may even need another doctor in the clinic before long."

"Gerard, I came here to say something, and if I don't say it now I may chicken out." She turned to face him.

"You never gave up on me, no matter how hard I was on you. And that made me realize if you didn't give up on me, then neither would God. Instead you were tender—some of the time—and patient—part of the time." She gestured toward the mission building. "I feel safer now than ever before."

"Careful about that. Remember the line in *The Lion, the Witch and the Wardrobe?* 'God is not always safe—'"

"'—but He's always good.' If you're trying to scare me off, stop it."

"Marriage to me might not be safe either," Gerard said gently, "but with you and me together, I know it would be good. We worked well together for nearly two years, Megan, but I want more than that with you. Marry me?"

She sighed. "You beat me to it."

He threw his head back and laughed. She reached her arms up around his neck and kissed him. "Why do you think I came all the way down here?"

He took her into his arms. "Let's be one another's port in the storm."

* * * * *

Dear Reader,

A couple of years ago I met a woman who has a heart that is very tender toward the homeless. She lives in Hollywood, and spoke to me about the growing number of homeless because of whole families losing their jobs. I got all excited about gathering a bunch of things together that those people might need, and sent them to her to pass out on the street. But as I sent them I realized it wasn't nearly enough. I wished I'd had more to do.

When I see something that touches my heart, I write about it in hopes that maybe it will touch the hearts of others who are like-minded. I realize that there are many homeless whose situations are almost hopeless, but there are also many who simply need a hand up, who have lost jobs, have too many bills, not enough money, or even lost unemployment income. So I dreamed about a homeless shelter and a hero who would be tough enough to handle all kinds of people, those who needed a hand up, and those who needed to learn to earn the food they eat daily. That's how Gerard developed in my mind. Then Megan developed when I wanted a physician who loved these hurting people with a great passion—a perfect partner for Gerard.

Recently I got excited when I read about a man who is doing exactly what Gerard does in this book—he puts people to work. No free handouts. Even if it's just sweeping the street, they earn their food. There is no better way to return a person's self-respect. Free handouts may be necessary for a time, but love comes when we care enough to help the needy rebuild self-esteem they may have lost when they forgot how to work for their food and shelter.

That's what Gerard Vance is all about. I'd love to see real people in real places doing this same thing. How about you?

Many blessings,

Hannah Alexander

Questions for Discussion

1. Dr. Megan Bradley breaks contact and abandons her post at the rescue mission in Corpus Christi to return to her hometown of Jolly Mill, Missouri. Her excuse is that the nightmares she was having were disturbing her neighbors. Does her reasoning seem rational to you when she still has nightmares about her patient's death?

2. Gerard Vance is so crazy about Megan that he makes plans to follow her to the place where she flees, and even establish a homeless rehab center and production plant there. How can you defend his outlandish actions?

3. Megan has been angry with God for a long time, and the anger only digs more deeply when she encounters the horrors of murder at the rescue mission. Have you ever been angry with God after a traumatic event? Have you ever felt He was punishing you?

4. The title of this story is *Eye of the Storm,* because Megan feels she may be hiding from the storm in Jolly Mill—she calls it the eye of her storm until she's called to find who may be killing her beloved friend, Kirstie Marshal. Have you ever gone through a storm such as hers? Gerard tells her she has been the eye of his storm—the breather he needed to get through it. God has been the eye of many of his storms. What has been the eye of yours? What got you through it?

5. Why do you believe Kirstie remained married to her husband despite the faithless acts she knew he was

involved in? How would you have handled such a relationship?

6. Megan doesn't appreciate Gerard tracking her down because she doesn't feel she can face what happened to Joni, but his presence helps her heal. Has someone ever done that for you by forcing you to face up to your fears? Please share.

7. Kirstie is erroneously diagnosed with premature Alzheimer's, which she rejects. Have you ever been misdiagnosed, misunderstood? Has your life been turned upside down because someone else tried to make you believe a lie?

8. Lynley is willing to give up her whole career to protect her mother, and Kirstie is desperate to make her daughter stop trying to protect her and live her own life. How would you handle this dilemma?

INSPIRATIONAL

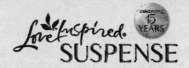

Love Inspired.
SUSPENSE

COMING NEXT MONTH
AVAILABLE APRIL 10, 2012

UNDERCOVER BODYGUARD
Heroes for Hire
Shirlee McCoy
With a stalker after her, Shelby Simons
needs a bodyguard—but does it have to
be this gorgeous former SEAL?

THE WIDOW'S PROTECTOR
Fitzgerald Bay
Stephanie Newton

RACE AGAINST TIME
Christy Barritt

AT ANY COST
Lauren Nichols

REQUEST YOUR FREE BOOKS!

2 FREE RIVETING INSPIRATIONAL NOVELS
PLUS 2 FREE MYSTERY GIFTS

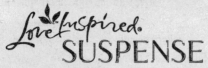

YES! Please send me 2 FREE Love Inspired® Suspense novels and my 2 FREE mystery gifts (gifts are worth about $10). After receiving them, if I don't wish to receive any more books, I can return the shipping statement marked "cancel". If I don't cancel, I will receive 4 brand-new novels every month and be billed just $4.49 per book in the U.S. or $4.99 per book in Canada. That's a saving of at least 22% off the cover price. It's quite a bargain! Shipping and handling is just 50¢ per book in the U.S. and 75¢ per book in Canada.* I understand that accepting the 2 free books and gifts places me under no obligation to buy anything. I can always return a shipment and cancel at any time. Even if I never buy another book, the two free books and gifts are mine to keep forever.

123/323 IDN FEHR

Name   (PLEASE PRINT)

Address   Apt. #

City   State/Prov.   Zip/Postal Code

Signature (if under 18, a parent or guardian must sign)

Mail to the **Reader Service:**
IN U.S.A.: P.O. Box 1867, Buffalo, NY 14240-1867
IN CANADA: P.O. Box 609, Fort Erie, Ontario L2A 5X3

Not valid for current subscribers to Love Inspired Suspense books.

**Are you a subscriber to Love Inspired Suspense
and want to receive the larger-print edition?
Call 1-800-873-8635 or visit www.ReaderService.com.**

* Terms and prices subject to change without notice. Prices do not include applicable taxes. Sales tax applicable in N.Y. Canadian residents will be charged applicable taxes. Offer not valid in Quebec. This offer is limited to one order per household. All orders subject to credit approval. Credit or debit balances in a customer's account(s) may be offset by any other outstanding balance owed by or to the customer. Please allow 4 to 6 weeks for delivery. Offer available while quantities last.

Your Privacy—The Reader Service is committed to protecting your privacy. Our Privacy Policy is available online at www.ReaderService.com or upon request from the Reader Service.

We make a portion of our mailing list available to reputable third parties that offer products we believe may interest you. If you prefer that we not exchange your name with third parties, or if you wish to clarify or modify your communication preferences, please visit us at www.ReaderService.com/consumerschoice or write to us at Reader Service Preference Service, P.O. Box 9062, Buffalo, NY 14269. Include your complete name and address.

LISUS11B

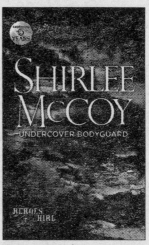

For a sneak peek of Shirlee McCoy's heart-stopping inspirational romantic suspense UNDERCOVER BODYGUARD, read on!

"It's okay," Ryder said, pulling Shelby into his arms.

But it wasn't okay, and they both knew it.

A woman was dead, and there was nothing either of them could do to change it.

"How can it be when Maureen is dead?" Shelby asked, looking up into his face as if he might have some way to fix things. He didn't, and he'd stopped believing in his own power and invincibility long ago.

"It will be. Eventually. Come on. You need to get the bump on your head looked at."

"I don't have time for that. I have to get back to the bakery. It's Friday. The busiest day of the week." Her teeth chattered on the last word, her body trembling. He draped his coat around her shoulders.

"Better?" he asked, and she nodded.

"I can't seem to stop shaking. I mean, one minute, I'm preparing to deliver pastries to my friend and the next she's gone. I just can't believe...." Her voice trailed off, her eyes widening as she caught sight of his gun holster.

"You've got a gun."

"Yes."

"Are you a police officer?"

"Security contractor."

"You're a bodyguard?"

"I'm a security contractor. I secure people and things."

"A bodyguard," she repeated, and he didn't argue.

Two fire trucks and an ambulance lined the curb in front of the house, and firefighters had already hooked a hose to the hydrant. Water streamed over the flames but did little to douse the fire.

Suddenly, an EMT ran toward them. "Is she okay?"

"She was knocked unconscious by the force of the explosion. She has a bad gash on her head."

"Let me take a look." The EMT edged him out of the way, and Ryder knew it was time to go talk to the fire marshal and the police officers who'd just arrived, and let the EMT take Shelby to the hospital.

But she grabbed his hand before he moved away, her grip surprisingly strong. "Are you leaving?"

"Do you want me to, Shelby Ann?" he asked.

"You can leave."

"I know that I can, but do you *want* me to?"

"I...haven't decided, yet."

Pick up UNDERCOVER BODYGUARD for the rest of Shelby and Ryder's exciting, suspenseful love story, available in April 2012, only from Love Inspired® Books Love Inspired® Suspense.